African Queen

Gallica quickened her pace. So did her pursuers. They began to stalk her. Knowing without a shadow of a doubt that she was their quarry, Gallica broke into a frenzied run and the threatening shout from behind made her realise the chase was on. They caught up with her in seconds; with a little whinny of fear she felt a hand going round her waist and she could smell the beer on their breath and the sweat on their bodies.

STARLING POINT 4

African Queen

Anthony Masters

Teens · Mandarin

To Vicky and Simon –
deeply loved, much
admired for their
devotion

First published in Great Britain 1990
by Teens
an imprint of Mandarin Paperbacks
Michelin House, 81 Fulham Road, London SW3 6RB

Mandarin is an imprint of the Octopus Publishing Group

Copyright © Anthony Masters 1990

A CIP catalogue record for this title
is available from the British Library

ISBN 0 7497 0195 1

Phototypeset by Input Typesetting Ltd, London
Printed in Great Britain
by Cox & Wyman Ltd, Reading

One

'Go for it.'

Naveed began to run up the Hill. It was a blazing hot May morning, and despite his shorts and singlet the back pack cut into his shoulders immediately. Not that there was much in it. Just a tracksuit, a pair of trainers and a couple of text books. The loose earth under his feet gave him the sensation of almost running on the spot, but because Dex was standing below him and shouting encouragement, Naveed ploughed on. Plough was the right word because the texture of the Hill was so loose – a mixture of sand and gravel – and it was hard to get a grip on its shifting surface. But there was no one except Dex to see him. It was Sunday morning and the school playing field was deserted.

'Go for it.' The voice came again, slow and steady, and Naveed went for it, looking up for a moment – something Dex had told him never to do. He soon realised that he wasn't going to be allowed to get away with it.

'Don't look up, you little prat.'

Naveed stumbled on, his breath coming in gasps

and his legs feeling like lead. The Hill seemed to grip at him, trying to pull him down into its soft spongy heart. He had trained hard, but it was only a week to the competition now and Naveed knew that this was one of the last days he would be able to put in any training.

'Go for it.' The words were fainter now, although Naveed guessed that he was only a quarter of the way up. His heart was pumping savagely and he tried to blot out the increasing pain by thinking of the good things – like the need to win and the fact that Dex was giving him his personal time. For last year Dex had run the Hill in the fastest time recorded for anyone in the school; now Naveed was determined to win the Junior Hill Climb Shield. His nearest rival was Jane Timpson, a cross-country runner of considerable stamina, and recently her timings had been much better than his.

The pain intensified as the sweat poured down Naveed's face. The grinding ache that seemed to be spreading all over him was almost unbearable. Was he improving on his timing? Why didn't Dex encourage him by telling him what the timing was? Suddenly he was full of resentment. The pain eased as he remembered what Dex had said a few minutes earlier as they had stood together, gazing up at the Hill in the nine o'clock sun. It would have been good to run in the cool of the dawn or the evening, but the competition was set in school time and Dex had insisted that they must simulate the conditions as exactly as they could. Naveed struggled on, and Dex's words came to him like pumping adrenalin, cool and sharp.

'You're going to do it, man. Sure as I'm going to my homeland. You're going to run that Hill and no one's going to catch you. Not Jane, not no one. You're going to be the Hill runner of the year. I say that on my mother's grave. And on Africa. The blessed land. I say it, man. You're gonna do it.'

The memory of the flood of words continued to douse him with renewed vigour, and then to his joy Naveed saw that he had just passed the blessed blue mark: halfway.

Mrs Newby was shaking with distress as she looked at the denuded front room. Her husband sat on the sofa, his head in his hands. The television and the video machine, the record player and cassette deck, and a whole load of electrical appliances had been stolen. Mick and Sharon stood there, wondering who could have been responsible for burgling their home. It was bound to have been an estate job, thought Mick, who had been in trouble himself and knew his way around the petty crooks on Starling Point. There had been a number of burglaries recently. The side window had been forced, and the thieves had entered with comparative ease for the back of the Newbys' flat overlooked the Wilderness – a piece of wasteland behind the estate. The Newbys had always bitterly regretted that the flat was in such a vulnerable position and Mr Newby had fitted all kinds of burglar alarms. But it looked as if either none of them had gone off or the burglars had had a special way of dealing with them.

The Newbys were devastated, not just at the loss but by the horrible feeling that strangers had desecrated their home. Sharon felt that she had been personally invaded while Mick's sense of outrage made him want to go out and thump someone. Mr Newby fulminated against the Starling Point estate and the 'vermin that lived on it' and Mrs Newby wept brokenly, repeating over and over again that she didn't deserve this and had never deserved it.

Naveed told himself that he must be nearing the top of the Hill now. He knew he had to keep going somehow whatever the pain, and he kept wiping the sweat out of his eyes only to have it pour in again. His whole body was full of weakness and water and there was a heaviness in his chest that seemed to be increasing. Despite the lightness of its contents, his back pack was now a complete dead weight and he was suddenly convinced he wasn't going to make it. All Naveed wanted to do was to lie down and hug the gritty sand and sleep for ever. But below him he could hear the insistent voice of Dex.

'Go for it. And don't stop. Go for it. Speed up. You've got to make it. Get on with it.' The exortations filled Naveed's mind and he staggered on somehow, not daring to look up or back – just watching the shining and unremitting surface of the Hill as it tormented him; a kind of slow-motion film that was mocking and relentless.

Next morning Mick was late for work in the super-market, but when Mr Dapor discovered the reason he was immediately sympathetic.

'These burglaries are really building up,' he said.

'They've always been around,' grunted Mick.

'Come in the stock room and have a cup of tea.'

'I'm O.K.'

But Mr Dapor was insistent. 'You've had a shock. Come and have something. Abdul can cope.'

'All right.' Mick grudgingly allowed himself to be fussed over, and once they were in the stock room and the kettle was on Mr Dapor started to talk about the rising crime rate on Starling Point. Mick sat there trying to relax and letting the words flow over him. But all he could feel was the hard lump of anger inside him. There was nothing that he wouldn't do to those burglars.

'They're on the increase, you know,' repeated Mr Dapor with gloomy relish as he poured out the tea, and Mick realised again how much Mr Dapor cared about his community.

Mick was very fond of his employer, who had given him a job at a very bad time of his life and had saved him from going inside. Now Mick was a trainee manager and he knew he was doing really well. Mr Dapor was thinking of opening another branch a few streets away and Mick had been told he was going to be the manager there if he continued to work so well. But this morning, because he was still in such a rage, Mick found it very difficult to listen to Mr Dapor. But listen he had to.

'They are on the increase right enough. I'm worried about my own premises. And I don't think the policing on this estate is sufficiently thorough. I'm going down the station to make a protest. I'm sure it's the kids from the Comprehensive who are responsible. That school has gone down so much since Imran's day that it's not the same place. I wish I'd never sent Naveed there.'

Desperate to divert him Mick said: 'Isn't your Naveed entered for that Hill sprint?'

As this was another subject that Mr Dapor disapproved of he was only too pleased to switch from one target to another.

'That headmaster. He's crazy. I don't want my son running up an artificial hill in all this heat.'

Mick grinned. Privately he thought the Hill was a good idea. Many of the Comprehensive pupils were utterly disillusioned with their lives, knowing they would leave school to face years of unemployment – or the kind of menial jobs that would gradually rot their souls. So, more for the thrill than anything else, they started stealing and vandalising, hacking away at the edges of their homeland. Mick understood their feelings well, because he had known the stale hell of unemployment himself.

Then Mr Wilks, the headmaster, had seen Sean Connery in a war film called *The Hill*, and it had given him sudden inspiration. He persuaded some local contractors to dump sand and gravel on a derelict part of the school playing field and gradually a sixty metre hill was constructed. It was a controversial idea and at first the education authority had tried to intervene and have the Hill removed, but when they realised what a challenge it was to so many frustrated and bored pupils the idea caught on and even the most disaffected wanted to take up the back-breaking, sweat-pumping challenge.

'It's dangerous,' protested Mr Dapor. 'It could give someone a coronary.'

'It's a good idea,' said Mick. 'Honest. It gives them a real thrill. I wouldn't mind having a go at it myself. Life can be so boring – day in, day out for those kids. But the Hill's given some of them at least something to go and take it out of.'

'Running up all that sand and gravel in this heat,' continued Mr Dapor. 'What does he think he is trying to do? Bring back National Service?'

'Maybe he does,' replied Mick. His thoughts returned to the devastated flat. If he had his way he would make those burglars run up the Hill twenty times a day until they dropped dead.

Naveed thought that he was going to drop dead any moment. He could hardly see for the sweat running into his eyes, his legs were incredibly heavy and a new pain in his chest was so tight that he could hardly breathe.

'Go for it.' He could hear the voice from the ground below and a breeze sprang up, soft and refreshing, and his breathing became just a little easier. Suddenly Naveed's feet seemed lighter and there was a spring in his stride that he hadn't felt since he began his ascent. Was this the second wind that he had heard so much about but never experienced before and had never really believed existed? Certainly it was a glorious relief and this time Naveed didn't take his eyes off the ground. He mustn't look up or maybe the pain would come back. This was the sixth time he had run the Hill and suddenly he had the feeling that he was doing better. Then the ground began to fall away beneath his feet and Naveed felt a burst of exhausted joy. He had done it! This must be the top. He allowed himself to look up. Yes – he was here. He was actually on top of the Hill. Naveed threw himself on to the shifting surface and yelled aloud in delight.

'Got it,' said the voice from below in triumph.

'How long?' Naveed managed to gasp out.

'Six minutes three seconds,' shouted Dex, and his voice rang with exultation.

Naveed gave another shout of joy. He had done it. He had smashed his own record by thirty-two seconds. His breath was coming in great pumping gasps and he ran the sand through his fingers. Then Naveed buried his face in the acrid surface and kissed it with his dry lips. Yes, he had done it all right. He sat up and looked down at Dex standing there below, glinting like some avenging warrior with his black skin shining in the sunlight and the dreadlocks round his shoulders. Naveed knew that without Dex's support he would never have climbed the Hill so fast. He forgot all about the agony as he sat there, looking down at the dusty grass. A little further away the four towers of Starling Point shone like a fantasy city, sparkling and gleaming in the sunlight that had never looked or felt so bright before.

'You staying up there all day?' yelled Dex.

Naveed hauled himself to his feet and with wild whoops of joy began to run down again. Then he tripped and rolled and was soon laughingly sprawled at Dex's feet.

Two

Gallica had gone to meet Leroy who was working on the Gallopers in Covent Garden. The Gallopers, a wonderfully old-fashioned roundabout with galloping horses, had first come to Starling Point with the fair. It had been magnificently restored and was now a real collectors' piece with its showman colours and ornate carving. Leroy had been overjoyed when Jim North, who owned the roundabout, first gave him the job of taking the money and maintaining the ride. He paid him generously and Leroy really liked him and his wife Gwen. But although he loved the job it had taken him away from Gallica and she had become so lonely she had started seeing Mick. But she knew – and Mick knew – that their temporary relationship was not working out and they were drifting apart by mutual consent. But although they had stopped being lovers, she and Mick were still friends and somehow they knew their friendship would continue, despite Mick's fiery temper. He was not jealous – he had always known it was inevitable that she and Leroy would come together again. Gallica had never felt so happy in her life and she was sure that despite

Leroy's travelling life with the Norths their love would now survive the separations. The evening they had just spent together seemed to be living proof of that; they had walked hand in hand through Hyde Park towards the cinema, completely absorbed in one another.

'I'd like to go to Jamaica,' he had told her. 'Just for a holiday. I could take you with me. I'm eighteen now and I've still never been there.'

'We could do that one year and then you could come to Africa.'

Leroy had grinned. 'At least you remember Africa and were born there, not on Starling Point like me. But my uncle said he would pay the fare and I could take a friend, so are you going to come with me or not?'

'You bet I am.'

Right now Gallica was very bored with her life – the only high point being the renewal of her friendship with Leroy. In the evenings she worked as the lowest of the low in a health club and she hated every moment of her fetch-and-carry existence. During the day she and Sharon sweated it out at sixth-form college, gloomily working towards their A-levels.

The walk through the park had been idyllic and Gallica and Leroy had promised each other the two trips over and over again. It was as if by separating and coming together again they were drawing even closer.

Gallica was so happy on the way back on the tube that she had hardly noticed the presence of the drunken football supporters. She was often nervous about travelling alone so late at night but this time she was so happy that she gave no thought to it at all. All she wanted to do was to stroll along the road back to Starling Point and dream about their future plans and savour their present happiness.

Absorbed in her own thoughts Gallica didn't notice the two middle-aged louts following her down the deserted road. It was unfortunate that she had decided to turn into the back entrance to the estate which led from a cul-de-sac into a narrow alley. It was only when she heard their raucous laughter that she turned and saw them grinning in the darkness. It was past midnight and there was no sign of anyone.

Gallica quickened her pace. So did her pursuers. They began to stalk her. Knowing without a shadow of doubt that she was their quarry, Gallica broke into a frenzied run and the threatening shout from behind made her realise the chase was on.

They caught up with her in seconds; with a little whinny of fear she felt a hand going round her waist and she could smell the beer on their breath and the sweat on their bodies.

'Come here, darling.' The heavy hands gripped her so firmly that she didn't even bother to struggle. She seemed frozen, unable to do anything else but stand there, terrified. They had both got hold of her now, forcing her up against a steel fence.

'Please,' Gallica whispered. 'Don't hurt me.' She could feel his hand riding up inside her skirt and she
16

began to scream. One of them produced a knife and held it at her throat.

'Don't make a noise. We're going to have a little bit of fun – that's all.'

The figure climbing out of the second-floor window dropped lightly on to the pathway in front of them. The boy was tall and black with his hair in dreadlocks and Gallica's two assailants immediately drew back, freeing her and leaving her to sob against the fence.

'What the hell do you want, you black bastard?' asked one of the men.

The kick was so quick that she hardly saw the black boy move his leg, but the man went down clutching his stomach. His companion hesitated, swore and then ran off as fast as he could. The boy heaved the other man to his feet, but as he did so he left himself unguarded and the man twisted quickly and punched him in the chest and then in the stomach. The boy fell to the ground gasping, and Gallica thought for a moment that she would be attacked again. But although the man looked at her with hungry, mocking eyes he turned away and ran after his companion, leaving Gallica bending over her rescuer.

'Are you all right?' she asked stupidly.

He squirmed and moaned and seemed incapable of saying anything at all. Then, very slowly, he sat up. He was extremely good-looking, she noticed, with high cheekbones and a long delicate face that gave no hint of his tough decisiveness.

'I'm all right.' He looked around him warily, then suddenly fell back again, clutching at his stomach. 'They done something to me.'

'You have to get to hospital.'

'No.'

'You must. He could have done something really nasty to you.'

He tried to stand up again – and fell back.

'Come *on.*' Her voice was urgent.

'I'm not going nowhere.'

'You *have* to.'

'No.'

She glanced at him curiously. 'Where did you spring from, anyway?'

He looked up at the flat above him. 'That's my nan's flat. I was watching telly and then I heard something. I looked out and saw those two blokes having a go. So I thought I'd better give you a hand.'

'I'm really grateful. They were going to rape me – I'm sure of it.'

He nodded and tried to stand for the third time. He failed.

'I'm going to get someone,' Gallica insisted.

'No.'

'There's a phone box just round the corner. I'm calling an ambulance.'

'Don't.'

'Why?'

'I'm scared of hospitals. Let me – the pain's going off a bit. Let me stand up.'

18

This time he made it, staggering shakily to his feet. 'I'm fine.'

'You're not. I think you've got a broken rib.'

'I'll be O.K.'

'Where do you live?'

'Other side of the estate.'

'Let me help you back.'

'Honest, I'll be all right. Where's your place?' He sounded impatient now.

'Just down the alley – it leads to the flats.'

'I'll see you back.'

'Are you at school?' Gallica asked as they moved off with the boy limping badly.

He shrugged. 'What's that to you?'

'I wanted to see you again and thank you properly. My boyfriend will, too. Can't we take you out for a meal?'

He grinned at her. 'No, thanks. Is this your place?'

'Yes.'

'In you go then.'

The boy watched her as she fumbled for her key and then opened the door of the ground-floor flat. Then he walked quickly away and disappeared into the dark concrete shadows around him.

Three

The next morning Mick Newby woke with a shattering headache and the realisation that he had done something wrong. Then he remembered what it had been. He had lifted five pounds from the till – something he had never done before. Of course, it would be all right, he told himself. Ted had paid him back the money he owed him in the pub – ten pounds in all, a fiver of which he would put back in the till first thing this morning. He had only lifted the money because he hadn't been sure that Ted *would* pay him back. He just couldn't have borne a dry night after the robbery. It would have been too depressing to stay in watching telly while his parents had bickered and bemoaned their fate. Nevertheless, Mick felt very guilty indeed about lifting the money, and swore that he would never do it again. Of course he could easily slip the note back into the till, but it was the principle of the thing that counted and he was *sure* that he wasn't going to do it again. Absolutely sure.

When Mick arrived at eight-thirty however there was an atmosphere in the supermarket. Mr Dapor seemed very remote and so was his wife. This was most unusual because they were normally very warm to him. He put the note back easily enough and began to work on the checkout. He didn't often do this now because he was training to be a manager, but Mr Dapor was insistent that he should be able to handle all aspects of the job.

At eleven, when he usually had a coffee break, Mr Dapor called Mick into the office. There was an ominous silence which seemed to Mick to last forever.

'Well, Michael?' Mr Dapor was looking at him very sadly.

'What's up?'

'You should tell *me* that.'

'Eh?' A sudden foreboding filled him.

'You should tell me what's up, as you say.'

'I'm not with you.'

'No? I'm sorry to hear that.' There was a long pause. Then he said: 'Have you done something that you are ashamed of?'

A cold chill stole over Mick. Did he know? *How* did he know? 'I don't know what you're on about.'

'I'm on about you taking money from the till.'

'I never.'

'We have a system of sometimes marking notes here, just to make sure that – all is well. It was your ill fortune that yesterday was one of our little checks. Last night the till was out of balance and this morning there was an unmarked note inside. You were the only person using that till yesterday and it was in balance the day before. Now have you anything to tell me?'

'Don't you trust your staff? I never knew you had this marking system.'

'It's just routine security.'

'You accusing me?' Suddenly Mick felt furiously angry. The police had spent hours at the flat yesterday and he still felt full of outrage at the burglary. Now here was Mr Dapor arguing over a trifle. It wasn't fair and he was damned if he was going to admit anything.

'No. I am *not* accusing you. Just asking you,' Mr Dapor said gently.

But Mick threw caution to the winds. 'Just because I was in trouble. You can't forget it, can you?'

'Mick, I have. That is all in the past. If you say you took nothing last night then I will accept your word. You're a management trainee – not a casual worker.'

But Mick, deeply guilty and upset, suddenly lost all control and began to shout at Mr Dapor: 'Stick you and your accusations.'

'I tell you: I am *not* accusing you.'

'I didn't take it. Right?'

'We will say no more about it.'

'I didn't take it and I want an apology.'

'I am sorry if I have upset you.'

'You don't believe me, do you?' he continued, his anger like fire in his brain.

'You've told me categorically that you did not take the money and I accept that. Shall we stop talking about it? You have my apology. Now let's say no more about it.'

Mick grunted and went back to work, but he was not appeased, despite the fact that he knew he was totally guilty. He was surprised at Mr Dapor's climb-down. He must really value me if he's prepared to apologise, one part of him told himself. But the other was full of grinding anger and that was infinitely stronger.

The tall boy walked into the supermarket at lunch-time when they were quiet and Mick was brooding behind the checkout.

'Do you have any Sparky Bubble Gum?'

'Sparky?' Mick looked up at him irritably. 'Never heard of it.'

'It's a new line.'

'Well, we ain't got it.'

'You sure?'

'Course I'm sure.'

'Only the thing is that my kid sister is dead keen on having some. She saw it on a telly commercial which said it was stocked in supermarkets everywhere.'

Mick sighed and then relented. 'I'll look in the stock room.'

'Thanks.'

Mick got up. There were a couple of customers looking in the freezers at the back of the shop but they didn't seem ready to check out yet.

'I shan't be a sec.'

'Right.'

He hurried into the stock room and scanned the shelves where new lines were put for Mrs Dapor to sort out. He rifled around but there was no sign of any new gum called Sparky.

'Sorry,' he said as he came out and sat down again at the checkout. 'We don't have any. Maybe it'll come in tomorrow.'

'She's always glued to that set — my kid sister.'

Mick gave him a thin smile and the tall boy with the dreadlocks said: 'I'll go down the road and see if the newsagent's got any.'

Mick yawned. 'You do that,' he said.

Gallica didn't go to school the next day. She had explained to her parents what had happened and they were horrified.

'You stay with me. Talk about it,' her mother had said. 'I don't want you bottling anything up.'

Gallica would have preferred to go to school and talk about the ordeal with her friends, but her mother was someone she *could* talk to so they spent most of the day thrashing it out and by the afternoon Gallica was feeling much better. She had been so tired after what had happened that she had slept without dreaming, so her experience had not stayed with her as much as she had feared it might.

She rang Leroy and felt instantly exhausted as she coped with his concern and anger and his desire to come over right away. Strangely, she would have wanted him to come at any other time, but today she desperately needed to be alone. There was one image she could not get out of her mind and she didn't know why. The face of the tall boy with the dreadlocks.

'This boy,' her mother was saying as they sat round the kitchen table having a comforting cup of tea, 'you mean he just came out of nowhere?'

'Out of his nan's flat, he said.'

'Well, it was a lucky break for you and all, my girl. And I tell you this – you're not walking home alone again. That I really mean. Leroy or no Leroy. Your daddy's going to meet you at the station whatever the time is – and you'd best not be too late again, anyway. Gallivanting about like that. I tell you –'

Gallica almost nodded off as her mother's voice drifted on and on. She would like to see the tall black boy with the dreadlocks again. Only to thank him, of course.

Mick was taking his afternoon tea break and was reading the paper in the stock room when Mr Dapor came in. Mick had been checking some accounts in the office during the afternoon and Mrs Dapor had taken over at the checkout.

'Michael.'

'Yes?'

'I have a problem.' Mr Dapor looked very weary.

'What's that?' said Mick in a surly voice. He was still feeling deeply guilty and depressed.

'There is more money missing from the till, and this time it's a lot.'

'What?' Mick looked up at him incredulously. 'How much?'

'About two hundred pounds.'

'Are you accusing me again?'

'No,' he replied patiently and cautiously. 'It's just that you were the last person on the till.'

'Your wife was.'

'You didn't sign off and cash up.'

'Sorry. I forgot.'

'That was unfortunate. My wife did and it turns out that there was two hundred pounds missing. I am only telling you and asking what you think we should do about it.'

But Mick was beside himself with rage once more. 'You accusing me?'

'Don't let's go through that routine again. Can we not just discuss the situation rationally.'

'You want to search me?'

Mr Dapor practically wrung his hands in front of him. 'Mick. Please.'

'You've branded me a thief. That's all you done.' He began to turn out his pockets. 'See, there's nothing there.'

'I'm going to have to report this to the police.'

'And me. I'm the first person they're gonna come looking for, aren't I? Me with my record. They're bound to suspect me.'

'Mick. This is the second time in two days. I can't afford to keep losing money. And this is a large sum. Are you sure you can't throw *any* light on all this?'

'No.'

26

'Are you sure?' Mr Dapor repeated sadly but Mick was on his feet. 'Where are you going?'

'Home.'

'But it's only half-four.'

'And you can stick your job.'

'What?'

'I just told you. You can stick your job. I'm not working anywhere where I've been accused of being a thief.'

'I'm not accusing you. You're a management trainee. I'm just asking you what you think we should do.'

'Call the Old Bill. They'll find me easily enough.' Mick pushed past him and walked out into the afternoon sunlight. He was shaking with a combination of rage and fear. He had just thrown away everything that had made his life worthwhile and he had no one to turn to. Sharon was wrapped up in her boyfriend Imran as usual, and it was ironic that Imran was Mr Dapor's eldest son. Still – that was how he had got the job in the first place. His parents were self-absorbed and almost hysterical over the burglary and he had even let Gallica go back to Leroy without putting up a fight. He had no one, no job – and no self-respect.

Four

'Mick.' She stood on her doorstep looking worn out.

He had been lying on his bed since he had returned home, full of self-pity. Then he had decided he must see Gallica.

'Come in. Mum's gone out to work and Dad's not in yet.'

'What's up?' he asked. 'You look knackered.'

'Thanks.' She paused and then it came out in a rush. 'I was attacked last night.' Her eyes filled with tears.

'What?'

'Someone rescued me.' She began to tell Mick the grim story as she led him into the sitting room. When she had finished Mick flopped down on the sofa and Gallica almost laughed. He was opening and shutting his mouth like a goldfish and he wore a look of punch-drunk surprise.

'Blimey. Are you all right?'

'They didn't hurt me. Didn't get a chance.'

'It's one thing on top of another.'

'Why?'

'We got burgled yesterday and I just walked out

of work this afternoon. And now you've been attacked. It's like the whole world's blown up.'

'You walked out of work?'

Mick told her why. When he had finished Gallica said, 'But he's not accusing you of anything.'

'He's having a damn good try.' Then Mick faltered. 'Have to tell you something, though.'

'What's that?'

'The fiver. I took it and I replaced it this morning. But I didn't touch the rest.'

'Why didn't you tell him?'

'How could I?'

'He's a good man. And you're a fool.'

'Thanks.'

'Well, you are. If only you had *told* him.'

'Well, I didn't, did I?'

They sat there, gazing hopelessly at each other. Then Gallica said: 'That two hundred –'

'Yes?' he asked guardedly. 'What about it?'

'When were you on the till?'

'All the morning.'

'Did you leave it?'

'No.'

'Are you sure?'

'Hang on. A young guy came in asking for some new bubble gum for his sister, and I went in the stock room to have a look and see if it was a new line.'

'How long were you gone?' she asked urgently.

'Couple of minutes.'

'Enough for him to put his hand in the till?'

'Maybe.'

'Who else was in the supermarket?'

'Couple of customers right at the back.'

'Any staff?'

'No.'

'Then he *could* have taken it. Do you remember what he looked like?'

'He was a tall black guy with dreadlocks.'

'Dreadlocks? How tall?' She stared at him in amazement and gathering concern.

'Pretty tall.'

'Did he have high cheekbones?'

'Can't remember. Why?' Mick stared at her wonderingly.

'Because he sounds just like the guy who rescued me last night. The guy who came out of a second-floor window.'

Mick looked up at her ashamed that he had hardly asked her about her attack.

Dex lay on his bed in the tower-block flat he shared with his mother. His stomach hurt less than it had the previous night and now it just seemed sore. He was nearly sixteen and in his last year at school. He had been born in Brixton and had never known his father. His mother Jessica was a croupier in a gambling club in Streatham and she seemed to bring home a different man each week, or sometimes twice a week. Dex was her only child and they rubbed along all right, moving from one flat to the other and sometimes from lousy digs to lousy digs from which they quite often had to do a moonlight flit. But Jessica had held the casino job down for three years now and they had been in Starling Point as long.

Dex's great love was sport. He was an excellent footballer as well as being a brilliant athlete. The school was rough and he had his fair share of fights, but ever since the Hill Dex had found a new joy. Despite his brilliance at athletics, he had never been consistent and had often dropped out of teams and training sessions, making himself unpopular with his peers and teachers alike. Before the Hill he hadn't cared; he just didn't have the will to see anything through. Home life was non-existent and although he was roughly fond of Jess, as he called his mother, and knew how lonely she was, he had always felt rejected by her. So the Hill had become a release and when Dex was angry, which was often, he would race up its shifting incline, feeling the heady pleasure of contesting his body with his will – which sharpened up as it won over his body. He also began to enjoy training some of the juniors who were keen on the competition that the Hill provided.

In particular, Dex had enjoyed training Naveed for the next Hill Sprint that was to be held in June. He found him very receptive and much more enthusiastic than anyone he had trained before. They had grown close during the training and Dex really felt that he had entered Naveed's mind sufficiently to will him to win.

But all this was really of the moment to Dex – a way of filling his time. Two years ago he had discovered the Rastas and his life had changed completely. Gradually he had become obsessed with the idea that England held no future for black people and their only hope was the foundation of an exclusive black society in Africa. He was heavily influenced by a local Rasta, Charles, who lived in a squat on the estate and who taught him that his life here was arid and hopeless – that the life of every black person outside Africa was arid and hopeless. And Dex, because he had nothing, was an eager, willing convert and soon all he could think of was Africa – and how he could get there. He did not exactly see it as a land of milk and honey and he knew that life would be difficult there. But Dex had an instinctive, sure and certain knowledge that he would belong there – that his roots were there – and that he had nothing here except an absentee mother, a dirty flat and the Hill.

For the last few months Dex had been saving up the money to go to Africa. He had visited a travel agent who told him that he would need at least three thousand pounds to get there and to live on until he could get a job. Dex decided to double the amount. At the moment he had two thousand pounds and he knew that he would be able to get the rest if his luck didn't run out.

For it was Dex – and Dex alone – who had been breaking into the flats at Starling Point, and by using a fence in Vauxhall he had done well. He was not a novice; Dex had been stealing on a small scale for years and he had plenty of criminal friends. Yes, he reassured himself, his luck should last long enough. Of course it would be lonely at first in Africa. Suddenly the face of the girl he had rescued last night swam into his mind. In fact, her face had been in and out of his mind all day. She had looked African. Perhaps he would get to know her and she would leave her boyfriend and come to Africa with him. He laughed – and winced with the pain of his bruised ribs. It was good to fantasise occasionally. When he had looked out of the flat he had been burgling and seen the girl struggling he had to take a very real decision. But Dex was not the kind of person to see someone hurt and he wouldn't hurt anyone himself – not if they were helpless. He just didn't have it in him.

'I'm not going back there.'

'You're an idiot.'

'Thanks.'

Gallica and Mick were having a major row. She wanted him to go back to Mr Dapor and admit the theft – and the return – of the five-pound note and then tell him about the boy who had come into the supermarket. The black boy with the dreadlocks. She knew that Mr Dapor was fair and would hear Mick out and probably believe him. By now, of course, the police might be involved and probably regarded Mick as a suspect. So Gallica felt it was vital that he moved quickly.

'The police will be looking for you,' she prompted again.

'Let them.'

'You're such a fool. They'll think you *did* it.'

'Let them.'

'He's a fair man.'

'Dapor's a bastard.'

'He's done a lot for you.'

'He patronised me.'

'It was just a very unfortunate incident. Please, Mick, go and see him.'

'No.'

There was a knock on the door and Gallica went to open it. On the threshold stood Mr Dapor. He looked nervous.

Gallica brought Mr Dapor into the sitting room before Mick could escape. As it was he was already in the kitchen trying to get out of the back door. But it was locked and he couldn't find the key. Grudgingly Mick returned to the sitting room and immediately became aggressive.

'I thought I might find you here. Your parents said I might when I went round to see them.' Mr Dapor's words tumbled over each other.

'You had no right.'

'I came to apologise.'

'*What*?' Mick sounded more furious than pleased.

'I should never have spoken to you in the way I did.'

'But you did – '

'What can I say? Please let me explain. My friend Mr Sharaz was outside the supermarket and he says he saw a black youth with dreadlocks hurrying out, at lunchtime, looking very suspicious indeed.'

'That proves nothing,' said Mick woodenly.

34

'He was in the supermarket,' explained Gallica. 'He asked Mick to see if some new chewing gum had come in and while Mick went to the stock room he must have pinched the money.'

Mr Dapor raised his hands. 'There you are, Michael. What did I say? I knew you were innocent.'

'You did *not*.'

'Mick, *please*,' began Gallica. But Mick was in no mood to be forgiving. He had been insulted and seemed determined to make the heaviest possible weather of it all.

'What happened,' he began in a measured tone, addressing Mr Dapor but looking at Gallica, 'was that you knew I'd been in trouble and because of that you immediately suspected me.'

'There *is* one thing,' Gallica intervened.

Mick turned on her. 'You shut your mouth.'

'I'm going to say it.'

'You do and I'll – '

Mr Dapor looked anxiously at both of them. What could they be talking about? And was someone going to get hurt?

'Mick borrowed a fiver yesterday and put it back this morning.' Gallica spoke hurriedly. 'He shouldn't have done it and he knows that and if he wasn't so angry then he would have told you himself. But I know that you are a really good person and would have understood.'

'Of course I would. We are all tempted and – ' began Mr Dapor.

But Mick was beside himself with rage and he

35

turned on Gallica. 'You stupid patronising girl. If I was going to tell him it would have been of my own free will and when I was ready. Now you've ruined everything.'

Gallica suddenly realised that she had been totally wrong in blurting it all out. She must have been crazy and of course Mick was bound to be livid. But she had wanted to help him.

Mick went up to Gallica and hit her savagely across the cheek with a tremendous crack and she staggered back amidst angry protests from Mr Dapor.

'Michael, what on earth are you doing? How dare you hit her?'

'I know what I'm doing. If *you* want some just say the word.'

'You can't *behave* like this.'

'I can. I am.'

'Michael – '

'Shut up.' He hurried out into the hall and threw open the front door. 'That will teach you not to interfere in my life,' he yelled at Gallica and slammed the door behind him.

Gallica burst into tears and Mr Dapor threw his arms round her.

'I shouldn't have said it,' she wept.

'It doesn't matter.'

'It *does*.'

'He'll come round.'

'Will you keep his job open?'

'Of course I will. He was doing so well and I never meant to patronise him. We have both mishandled

Michael. But it is only because we are both so fond of him.'

'The trouble is,' said Gallica, wiping her eyes. 'The trouble is that Mick has always been a walking time bomb. And now we've set him off.'

'Rubbish,' said Mr Dapor. 'You see. He'll be back and he'll be sorry.'

'That's the one thing that Mick can never be.' She began to cry again. 'He can never admit that he's wrong.'

Five

Mick had decided to get drunk and then realised that he hardly had a penny on him. So he walked the streets around Starling Point for hours and it was midnight before he decided to return home. But the walk hadn't cooled him down in the slightest and he was still boiling with continually recharging rage. The burglary, the accusation in the supermarket and now the way Gallica had so thoughtlessly given him away were all too much for Mick to bear. He kicked at the wall and hurt his foot, staggering around for a while cursing. Then he turned and came face to face with the boy he had seen in the supermarket – the tall black boy with the dreadlocks. It was like magic. Like heavenly justice.

'You!' he yelled.

The boy took one look at Mick and began to run. But Mick was too quick and jumped on him. They swayed and then fell to the ground. No one saw them struggling for they were near the Wilderness and B Block – the section of Starling Point used for emergency accommodation which was often half empty.

Mick and Dex rolled across the concrete. Mick

could feel that his opponent was every bit as strong as he was – if not stronger. For a while they continued to roll about on the ground, trying to punch and kick at each other but in fact doing very little damage. Then suddenly the boy was on top of him and Mick could not get him off. He was punching at his chest and face and it was only Mick's anger that gave him the extra strength he needed to kick him away and then, with a twist, leap on top of him. Somehow he managed to pin Dex down, but it seemed a very long time before he stopped struggling. Eventually he was still.

'You nicked that money,' snarled Mick.

'Dunno what you mean,' panted Dex.

'I mean you nicked that two hundred.' Mick hit him hard in the mouth and saw the blood flow from Dex's lips. 'Want another?'

'Bastard.'

'I said – want another?'

Dex tried to throw Mick off but he was in too commanding a position.

'You going to tell me?' demanded Mick, hitting him again.

'All right.'

The sudden capitulation unnerved Mick and he pressed down harder, wondering if his sudden acquiesance was a trick. But it didn't seem to be.

'You're hurting me.'

'That's the idea.'

'O.K. I took it. But you're not going to nick me.'

'Why not?'

'Because I could cut you in.'

'Eh?'

'Cut you in. That two hundred quid. It's only a beginning.'

'Beginning of what?'

'That Paki takes a lot of money at that supermarket. I'm gonna do him. While he's walking down the bank. I mean – I know you work there, but that Paki deserves – '

'Don't insult him.' Mick grabbed Dex's dreadlocks and lifted his head. 'Or I'll break your skull.'

'Wait – '

But Mick had suddenly thought of something. 'Hang on. You been breaking in anywhere else?'

'Yeah.'

'You been to the Grove flats?'

'Only the other night.'

'Nineteen?'

'Could be.'

Mick yanked at Dex's dreadlocks and he let out a howl of agony.

'That was my place you did.'

'I'm sorry.'

'They're looking for you for that.'

'I didn't leave any prints.'

'I'm going to march you down the nick.'

'You can try.'

'I don't care how hard it is, or what sort of fight you put up. And when I do get you down there you're going to tell them everything.'

'So no cut?'

'No way. You should have seen my folks. You should have seen them.'

'I said I'm sorry.'

'Sorry. What do you mean, *sorry*?'

'So the cut's out. Just because I did your place.'

'Shut up.'

'I'm doing another job. And it's going to be that supermarket. Wouldn't you like to have a go at that Paki?' said Dex persuasively, trying to prevent Mick from shopping him.

'He's a good guy. You touch his place and I'll kill you.'

'Suppose we try somewhere else?' Dex was getting desperate now.

'We?'

'Just one big job. You and me could make a good team.'

'I don't want no more thieving.'

'I could set you up for a long time. What about the Cash and Carry? In Sunderland Street. That's an easy one.'

The temptation blazed across Mick's mind. What the hell did it matter what he did? No one respected him anyway and he was always going to be the chief suspect for everything. Why not give them something really big to chew on?

'How are you going to do it?' he asked.

'So you're interested?'

'I haven't said so yet.'

'Let me up.'

'When you tell me.'

'All right. I was going to go there tomorrow about five and stick them up.' In fact Dex had no such intention, but if only he could get Mick off him he would have a chance of running for it. And if he got a start, he didn't think Mick could catch him. Not this time.

'Are you crazy?'

'I've got a mask,' Dex lied.

'You must be barmy.'

'Can't you take a risk? I stick them up and we do a runner.'

'You actually expecting me to join you?'

'Why not? Could be a couple of grand each.'

'Go and take a jump.'

'Can you drive?'

'Yeah.'

'Got wheels?'

'No.'

'I can get some.'

'I'm no getaway driver.'

'What more can I offer you?' asked Dex.

Mick got up and hauled Dex to his feet. 'You some kind of fantasy merchant?' he said scornfully. 'More likely you're just trying to trick your way out of this.'

'No.'

'I'm going to take you down to the nick either way.'

'For God's sake. I've offered you what I can.' Dex was panicking now. There was no doubt that Mick really meant it.

'Shut up.'

Dex began to struggle again and Mick hit him. He staggered to a side wall and then aimed a running kick at Mick which missed.

'O.K. Stop where you are.'

They stopped and froze as two policemen emerged from the shadows.

Gallica eventually phoned Leroy in the caravan that he shared with the Norths. She knew that she should have done so before but for some reason that she could not admit to herself, she had put off making the call time after time.

'Mick's in trouble,' she said.

'Again?' Leroy's voice was cynical.

'Don't be rotten. That was all over eighteen months ago.'

'Was it now?' She knew that Leroy had very little sympathy for Mick, who had once been involved in vandalising his beloved roundabout. And although it had been Leroy who broke up their first friendship because of his work on the fairground, she knew that he had been very unhappy about her seeing Mick. Because of this she had never told Leroy that she had slept with Mick. Gallica didn't think it would do them any good and he had never directly asked. But she sensed the tension every time Mick's name came up.

'What's happened?' he asked, feigning an interest.

'Mr Dapor suspected that he might have stolen some money from the till, but now it looks as if someone else did it.'

'So?'

'Mick was offended and walked out.'

'He's like that.'

'But I've made it worse.'

'How?'

'Well. He *did* lift a fiver earlier and he put it back. But Mr Dapor marks some of the notes and Mick denied all knowledge of pinching the money. Then someone else came in and nicked two hundred quid. The trouble is I told Mr Dapor about the fiver – in front of Mick.'

'What the hell did you do that for?' Gallica instantly felt much worse. If even Leroy disapproved then she must have been really stupid.

'I thought it would bring everything out into the open and Mr Dapor was very nice. But Mick – '

'Wasn't,' said Leroy abruptly and Gallica felt her explanation to be even lamer.

'He ran out.' She decided against telling him that he had slapped her.

'Where to?'

'I don't know. I phoned his mum but he hadn't been home. And they've just been burgled and all.'

'It sounds like a real soap opera back at Starling Point. What am I missing?'

'Me?'

'A lot. *You* know that.'

'Do you mind me ringing late like this?'

'Not a bit.'

'What am I going to do about Mick?'

'Stop trying to mother him.'

'I thought you might say something like that.'

'You think I'm jealous of the guy?'

'You might be.'

'I probably *am*,' he said, considering. 'But not that much. He's a born loser.'

'That's not fair.'

'I don't want you mixed up with him.' Leroy's voice took on a sanctimonious note.

'You don't own me.'

'Who said I did? I just love you, that's all.'

'Leroy – I'm sorry – ' Gallica began.

'Go to bed and sleep on it.'

Now she felt that he was patronising her and a tiny spark of resentful anger flared inside her. 'It *won't* be better in the morning,' she snapped.

'*You* might be. And then you're coming up on Tuesday. I thought we'd eat Chinese. Maybe take in a movie.'

'Great.'

'How are my folks?'

'Your parents are fine.'

'And that little sod of a kid brother of mine?'

'He's fine, too.' But all the time they were talking the spark of anger gradually grew into a flame. How dare he patronise me? she thought. And treat Mick like dirt. In her mind's eye, however, she was not looking at Leroy – or Mick. She was looking at her gallant knight – who was also a thief. The boy with the dreadlocks.

'I want *you* to be fine, too,' said Leroy abruptly.

'I will be,' she replied vaguely.

45

'Don't get mixed up with that Mick.'

'I love you.' But Gallica's voice lacked warmth and Leroy hastened to compensate.

'If you're unhappy phone me any time. Jim can always fetch me.'

'Bye.'

'Bye, love. And take care.' By this time, Leroy was feeling both puzzled and worried, but Gallica had gone.

'Having a bit of a scrap, were we?' asked the copper.

'I was making a citizen's arrest,' said Mick with determined dignity.

'You were, were you? Don't I know you? Isn't it Mick Newby?'

'Yeah.'

'And your friend – introduce me to your friend.'

'He's no friend of mine.'

The policeman flashed his torch in Dex's face. 'Who are you, son?'

'Dex Warren.'

'You sure about that?'

'Want to wake up my mum? She'll tell you.'

'You local, then?'

'Yeah.'

'So what's going on?'

'He burgled my place and then he nicked some money from the supermarket and they thought it was me,' said Mick in a great rush.

The other copper grinned. 'Oh, yeah?' he said sarcastically.

'What are you grinning about?' said Mick indignantly.

'Nothing.'

'So what was the scrap about?' asked his companion.

'I told you,' snapped Mick. 'I was going to take him down the nick and make a citizen's arrest, only he didn't fancy the idea much.'

'He jumped me,' said Dex.

'Because I recognised you,' insisted Mick.

'O.K. What's your story, Warren?'

'Him and me was thieving together. We was a team.' Dex was thinking desperately fast and Mick looked decidedly unhappy. 'We did a couple of houses and then we did the supermarket. He was on the inside, like.'

'You bloody liar,' swore Mick, advancing on him threateningly. Meanwhile Dex was working at the story. If he could just keep them talking long enough he could run. And he could get the money from its hiding place and sleep rough and do over some more houses and get more money and then set off for Africa. He just had to keep them talking. A wave of panic swept him as he suddenly realised how much he was fantasising.

'Yeah. He was in on it from the beginning. In fact, he put me up to it and that's why we were having the bundle.'

Mick launched himself at Dex in fury and the policemen made the mistake of both grabbing hold of him. Dex needed no second chance. He was gone in a flash. One of the policemen immediately stopped wrestling with Mick and gave chase, but it was too late. Dex could run like lightning and the policeman was soon puffing in his wake and watching him disappear into the night. He trailed back to his colleague and swore.

'Never mind. We got one of them.'

'He was lying,' yelled Mick. 'I never did nothing. I was making a citizen's – '

'We'll sort that out down the nick,' said the copper firmly and put him in a half-nelson.

Six

Sharon met Gallica on the way to the Saturday morning job she had in a florist. Sharon looked distraught and Gallica knew that it had to be something to do with Mick.

'Did he get back last night?'

Sharon shook her head. 'He was nicked – and *then* sent home,' she said miserably and Gallica's heart plummetted.

'Why?'

'I don't know. Dad's going crazy. It's something to do with all the burglaries we've been having on the estate.'

'But Mick can't be mixed up in those.' Gallica was horrified. 'I mean – one of them was your house.'

'I know.'

'But he *can't* have done it.'

'They've charged him,' said Sharon bleakly. She began to sob and Gallica put her arms round her.

'They said something about him beating someone up when they arrested him,' said Sharon through her tears. 'Another boy who ran off. They reckon he was in it with Mick. Or that's what Dad says.'

'But you can't believe all this?' Gallica was angry now – an anger propelled by fear.

'I don't know what to believe.'

'But he wouldn't have burgled his own house. It's ridiculous.'

'The detective told Dad that he might have done that to put everyone off the scent. They found an envelope on him. There was two hundred pounds in it and Mr Dapor has identified it as his money.'

'I don't believe it.' But Gallica was filled with a dreadful foreboding.

'Neither do I. But it looks bad.'

'I have to see him,' said Gallica.

'Mum and Dad may not let you in.'

'They'll have to,' Gallica replied defiantly.

In the end they did, but only after a good deal of persuasion. Mrs Newby was tight-lipped and disapproving while Mr Newby's face was set. He was disgraced – his son had robbed his own home. It just didn't bear thinking about.

'O.K. Five minutes,' said Mr Newby. 'But he's really gone and done it now. I always knew he was no good.'

Mrs Newby said nothing – it was as if she could not trust herself to speak. Gallica could see tears in her eyes and knew why.

'Since you're here,' said Mr Newby brusquely, 'you might as well try and get the truth out of him. We can't.'

Mick was in the front room and, mercifully, they

were left alone together. He looked awful, with bloodshot eyes and bruises all over his face.

'Mick.' She stretched out a hand to him and Mick took it like a young child.

'I didn't do it.' He was close to tears. 'I just didn't do it.'

'I know you didn't,' she said firmly.

But he looked at her strangely. '*How* do you know?'

'Because I know you. That's why.'

'You heard what they charged me with?' His voice rose to a high aggrieved note and Gallica realised he was almost out of control of himself.

'No.'

'Burglary and other things. God knows what things.'

'You *didn't* do it. They'll drop the charges.' She felt she was speaking as naively as she had to Mr Dapor.

'Don't be a fool,' said Mick sharply.

'I'm sorry.' Gallica looked away, feeling totally inadequate.

'You heard about the money?'

'Yes.'

'He must have planted it on me.' And he briefly told her the story. 'He either stuck it in my pocket during the fight or when the coppers turned up. God knows how he did it. But he did it all right and he's stitched me up good and proper.'

'They'll find him.'

'Will they? And even if they do it's only his word against mine.' Mick's voice was bitter.

'You got a lot of supporters.'

'Who?'

'There's me and Mr Dapor.'

'Dapor? Not after his two hundred was found on me.'

'I'm sure – '

'Yeah. You say he's a fair man. But he won't be so fair now he's found out about the money.'

'We'll get you out of this, Mick. I promise. I *know* you didn't do it.'

He suddenly leant forward, all cynicism gone. 'Do you mean that?'

'I mean every word of it. I'll clear you. We'll all clear you. Somehow.'

'*Promise* you believe me?'

'I promise,' she said. Now that he was so helpless Gallica was feeling stronger and she knew she had to stay that way.

On the way out only Mrs Newby stood in the hallway.

'Well – ' she blurted out. 'What did he say?'

'He said he didn't do it,' replied Gallica.

Mrs Newby looked at her cynically but there was something else in her eyes. A kind of wild hope?

I've stitched him up good and proper, thought Dex, but it brought him little comfort. He lay on the filthy floor of the squat, knowing that the police had searched it last night and would be unlikely to do so again. He wanted to stay at Starling Point for at least one more day for suddenly, surprisingly, he was determined to say goodbye to his mother. He had thought little about her for all these years, but now Dex had a burning urge to see her and take her in his arms. He knew that it was dangerous to hang around, but it would also give him one more day of normality before he was forced to move on and bring the two long years of his Rastafarian ideals to fruition.

The squat was in a small six-storey block on the very fringe of Starling Point. Around it was the emergency accommodation whose tenants were largely composed of what the local authority described as problem families: people down on their luck and some of the single homeless who had drink problems.

Charles and Sammy – two Rastafarians Dex had known for some time – had originally lived a few streets away, but one night they had broken into a deserted flat on the block and made it their home. Charles was middle-aged and a severe asthmatic and his common-law wife Sammy looked after him. But both really lived in their minds. It was through them that Dex had been introduced to the Rastafarian movement in the first place. Charles said he would never live to see Africa but Dex wondered whether that was because he preferred to dream about it.

All the money Dex had stolen was hidden in the Wilderness in an old air-raid shelter where he had made a kind of false floor, and neither Charles nor Sammy had the faintest idea about his rampage of burglaries. Dex had told them that his uncle was lending him the money to work his way over on a cargo boat. It all sounded a bit romantic but they seemed to swallow the story, although Dex suspected that they were so outside the real world they would have swallowed anything. The sounds of Bob Marley, the Rastafarian singer, continually echoed around the rooms of the squat and the smoke and muzziness of ganga ensured Utopia for Charles and Sammy.

Fellow Rastas would often come to the squat, as well as Janata, a male nurse who was a friend of Imran and Mick. Janata, however, had no interest in ganga or Africa. He simply came in every day to care for Charles. Janata was HIV positive and they all knew he was taking a great risk with his health by coming into the dirty squat. His whole immune system was breaking down and a cold could easily turn into pneumonia. But despite the risk Janata still came, and although he had been a psychiatric nurse, he would help Charles by giving him breathing exercises and fetching his medicines from the chemist, particularly when Sammy was high on ganga and incapable of helping anyone. Charles and Sammy had grown very fond of Janata and had no inhibitions about his disease, and neither had Dex.

His need for sanctuary was the reason Dex gave to Charles and Sammy for coming to stay with them at the squat. He explained that he was now on the run after getting mixed up in a fight with Mick Newby and the police were accusing them of both being mixed up in burglaries that Dex assured them he did not commit. And of course they believed him, because they never questioned anything in their lives.

Janata cautiously let himself in round the back of the squat bringing the sweets that Sammy was addicted to. She seemed to have stopped in a time warp, for although she was middle-aged she still acted like a young girl living in the sixties.

'How are you, Charles?' asked Janata, peering into the smoky gloom.

'Not so good today. The heat makes me wheeze.' He was a great broken giant of a man with huge shoulders and a straggling beard. Charles had been teacher and mystic, hospital porter and merchant seaman. Now he was a philosopher.

'I've brought you the ventolin.'

'Thank you.'

'Where's Sammy?'

'Taken to her bed. She has a bad head.'

Janata turned to Dex. 'It's all over the grapevine that you're on the run. What did you do?'

Dex explained patiently, making sure that what he told Janata was what he had told Charles. Not that it really mattered, for Dex was sure that Charles had not taken much in.

'You still at school?' asked Janata.

'Was. Before all this happened,' replied Dex almost wistfully.

'Do you know what they're saying on the grapevine?'

'I don't want to know.'

'But I do,' said Charles, and there was a sudden steeliness in his voice that Dex had never heard before and did not like. Would he ever consider giving him up? A fellow Rasta? He had relied totally on Charles's other-worldliness and now it looked as if he had been wrong. Like he had been wrong about not wanting to see his mum. Suddenly Dex's world seemed to be in pieces and he didn't know what he wanted any more.

'They're saying that you were carrying out burglaries with Mick Newby. And that you grassed him and ran away.'

'Rubbish,' said Dex unconvincingly.

'That's what they're saying,' said Janata flatly and Dex cursed him inwardly for his interference.

'This true, Dex?' asked Charles.

'No, it's not true.' But again his voice sounded wrong.

There was another long silence then Charles said: 'You're not letting another guy take it for you, are you, Dex?'

Suddenly a pit opened in Dex's mind. He realised that he had been living in a fantasy world for a very long time. He had stolen two thousand pounds and stashed it away in the Wilderness and that had been his African dream money. He thought of his mum again and realised he didn't want to go to Africa after all. Dex looked up at Charles like a helpless child.

'Dex,' said Charles with a new and commanding authority.

'Yeah?'
'What you been doing?'

Seven

Naveed walked home from Urdu class slowly and alone. It was on the grapevine. Dex was on the run from the police. No one had said anything officially but he trusted his sources. His sense of loss was enormous, for without Dex he knew that he would never win the Hill sprint. There was only a week to go and without Dex he was sure he would stand no chance.

Dex was all the things Naveed wanted to be. A wonderful athlete, popular with girls – above all a free spirit with his longing for Africa which he had often talked to Naveed about. And as far as he himself was concerned, apart from the tortures and exhilaration of the Hill, Naveed found himself a prisoner, shackled to his home and his religion – which really amounted to the same thing. His brother Imran had forsaken Islam many years ago and had a white girlfriend – Sharon – a relationship of which their surprisingly tolerant parents approved. They had been deeply upset when Imran left his religion – a way of life for any Muslim – for his parents were devout. Until now he had been the same, but at fourteen he was beginning to resent the way he had almost become a prisoner to Allah with prayers five times a day and Urdu classes all over the weekend as well as the mosque. Naveed screamed to break out. By contrast Dex was free and he wanted to be with him.

Now, without Dex saying 'Go for it', the Hill was nothing. Nothing at all. Yet as he walked home alone, Naveed suddenly could not bear his pre-ordained existence any longer and he turned and ran back to the Hill.

It was a still May afternoon and the sun was warm but not hot. Between the school and Starling Point was a small and dusty park and he could see mothers and their children near a sandpit and a few old people walking their dogs. There was a steady stream of traffic on the road but the school playing field was deserted. Naveed had decided to train on his own and try to hear Dex's voice in his mind.

Dex told them everything, and Charles and Janata listened quietly without interrupting. When he had finished Janata said: 'There are other ways of raising money for Africa.'

'What ways?' asked Dex bleakly. He was in their hands now – their responsibility – and he was scared for the first time in his life.

'You could be sponsored.'

Dex said something very rude. Then Charles spoke for the first time: 'We can't shelter you here, Dex.'

'I know that now.'

'We are at risk enough. And, of course, you are bringing discredit to the movement.'

Dex said nothing.

'So I think you should give yourself up. And let this white boy off the hook, too.'

'I'll be put away.'

'We can support you in court,' said Janata. 'There are extenuating circumstances.'

'Yeah.'

'I can help you.' Janata's voice was urgent but Dex's mind was a wasteland. No Africa. No freedom. Just being locked away.

'And I would if I could,' said Charles. 'But I wouldn't cut much of a figure of respectability in court.'

'You wouldn't,' Dex agreed. But what about Janata? Would the court think Janata was only appearing because he fancied him? Would they know he was gay? Dex felt utterly confused.

'So what are you going to do?' asked Charles.

Dex knew what he had to do. Being on the run was impossible now. He wanted to own up and he wanted everything to be all right again. But he knew that it wouldn't. Africa was now only the fantasy that in fact it had always been, and the two thousand pounds in the air-raid shelter an appalling liability. He stood up. 'I'll go and collect the money and go up the nick.'

'Shall I come with you?' asked Janata.

'No,' said Charles. 'I'll go with him. He's a Rasta,

and although I may be no good in court at least I can support him now.'

'Thanks, Charles,' said Dex. He turned to Janata. 'What do you mean "extenuating circumstances"?' He felt he was clinging to a straw.

'I mean that your home life hasn't always been what it could be and you've done superbly at sport at school. They'll say you have potential. And what about Naveed and the Hill? That's a really imaginative scheme and Mr Dapor – the man you nicked the money off and planted on Mick Newby – he may put in a word for you; after all, his son is more important to him than two hundred pounds.'

'But they're very strict Muslims. He won't back a thief.'

'You don't know him. He's one of the good guys.'

A tiny spark of hope rose in Dex's heart. 'You reckon?'

'I reckon.'

Dex turned to Charles. 'Let's go then.'

'I'm not your keeper. Do you *want* me to come?' asked Charles insistently.

'Yes – I want you to come. We'll get the money first. Then we'll walk to the nick. But there's just one place I want to see on the way.'

'What's that?'

'The Hill. It reminds me of freedom and of Africa. I just want to see it.'

'We'll see it then,' said Charles firmly.

Naveed tried to hear Dex's voice in his mind as he

pounded and gasped his way up the Hill. But he couldn't hear him at all and he kept looking up and doing all the things that Dex had told him not to do. He didn't measure his pace nor did he count his steps, and as a result his exhaustion was so great that he suddenly lay down halfway up the ascent. He pressed his face into the hot and dusty surface and began to cry. Dex, he said in his mind time and time again. Dex, where are you? I can't do it without you. Then he heard a voice, which at first he thought was some kind of mocking fantasy.

'Go for it. Get up and go for it.'

He stirred and looked round and there to his amazement stood Dex with an old man with a beard and Rasta dreadlocks and a long black coat. He looked like a tramp. Amazed, Naveed struggled to his feet and stared down.

'I said, go for it and stop going to sleep on the job,' Dex yelled up at him.

Naveed turned and began to run.

Naveed stood on top of the Hill, feeling liberated and full of joy. He waved down and Dex waved back. Then Naveed began to run down as fast as his legs could carry him. He fell into the strong wiry arms of Dex and they hugged each other.

'Now,' said Dex. 'We're going to do it together.' He looked at Charles and he nodded.

'All right. Just the once.'

Dex and Naveed began to run side by side. To Naveed it was as if his feet hardly touched the ground. His thoughts began to keep pace with his running and the strain just wasn't there. He became more and more light-footed. Dex ran beside him, and Naveed had the extraordinary feeling that they were sharing the same pair of lungs. Together they were a pair of magnificent running machines that were scaling the heights of the Hill with ease and style and a joyous sense of freedom. A little breeze stirred about them and magically this seemed to ease them along their way. The air tasted delicious, slightly salty and scented with newly-mown grass. The sweat on Naveed's brow was light and cooling and he rejoiced in the flying of his feet. Then, with remarkable suddenness, they reached the top and threw themselves down. Turning, they could see Charles looking up. He was smiling. They lay there for a while with the breeze caressing their bodies and then Dex sat up. Sensing that he had something to say, Naveed sat up too and the breeze that had been so gently cooling suddenly seemed cold.

'Naveed.'

'Yes?' he asked apprehensively.

'I've enjoyed this. Enjoyed doing the training. All of it. But I've done something wrong that I don't want to talk about and I have to go down the nick and they'll probably send me down.' Dex brought it all out in a rush and Naveed listened, hardly taking it in.

'How long will you be away?'

'It could be a long time.'

'So you won't be here for the competition?'

'No.'

Naveed burst into tears.

'Don't cry.'

'I want you to be there.'

'I can't. And you're making it worse.'

But Naveed continued to cry.

'Please stop.'

Naveed tried rather unsuccessfully and his sobs were hard and dry.

Dex put an arm round him. 'I want you to promise me something.'

'What?'

'I want you to win the sprint.'

'How can I? Without you?'

'You can hear my voice.'

'How can I?'

'In your mind.'

'I tried before. It wouldn't come.'

'You must try *harder*. I'll be thinking about you. Willing you.'

Naveed nodded.

'I could send you a tape, maybe. But mainly I'll be thinking. Willing you.'

'Yes.'

'*You* have to help.'

'I'm trying.'

'You're going to be free — I'll be locked up.'

'Aren't you going to Africa anymore?'

'You bet I am. But it's going to be delayed.' He tried to make his voice reassuring, so that Naveed still had something of his image to cling on to.

'When will you come out?'

'I don't know. But you're lucky. You *have* to win because you're free.'

'I'm not. I have to go to the mosque and Urdu classes and pray five times a day.'

'Yeah, and I'm going to share a cell and be banged up most of the day. How would you like that?'

Naveed shook his head. Then Dex stood up.

'I've got to go.'

'Where you going?' asked Naveed naively.

'Down the nick.'

'I want to come with you.'

'No.'

'Please.'

'I don't *want* you to come. It would upset me too much, man. I'm going with Charles.'

'Who's he?'

'An old mate. A Rasta.'

'What shall I *do*?'

'I want you to have another practice. Now.'

'I'm too tired.'

'You're not. And you have to practise something else.'

'What?'

'Listening to my voice.'

Charles shuffled along very slowly towards the police station but Dex didn't mind. He looked round at the littered streets and the battered shop fronts, wanting to savour the familiar scene as long as he could. He waved to a mate and grinned at a girl he knew, but

65

slowly, irrevocably, they came to the road that led to the police station and then he could see the old Victorian building. Dex felt that he was sentenced already.

Maybe they would nick him before he got there, for after all they were meant to be searching for him, weren't they? But the station loomed nearer and nothing happened. They crossed the road and passed within a few centimetres of a copper, but he showed not the slightest hint of recognition.

'Are you ready?' asked Charles.

'I'll never be ready.'

'You'll get to Africa.'

'Do I want to?'

Charles looked away and Dex could feel a bitter disappointment radiating from him. 'I'm coming in with you and I'll wait with you as long as I can.'

'Thanks.' Dex's voice shook. 'Thanks a lot, Charles.'

'We're fellow Rastas. We support each other.'

'You bet we do.'

Just as they were about to walk up the steps to the police station Dex heard a shout behind him. He turned and saw that it was Naveed, still in his running gear.

'I did it!' Naveed yelled across the road at him.

'What?' Dex was momentarily confused.

'I beat my best time on the Hill.'

'Did you hear my voice?'

'Yeah. That's how I did it.' They were both shouting above the traffic.

'You have to keep improving on your time.'

'I will.'

'Hear my voice.'

'Always. I'm coming across. I want to see you in.'

'No. I told you – no.'

'I'm coming.'

'No.'

But Naveed, looking neither to right nor left, hurled himself across the road. The bus struck him as he was halfway across.

Eight

The screaming of brakes seemed to fill the entire street. Dex and Charles stood frozen on the steps of the police station. Naveed was being literally bounced down the road and he rolled over and over as if he would never stop. Then they heard his skull hit the kerb with a resounding crack.

Dex leapt from his frozen position on the steps of the police station and tore back across the road to where Naveed was lying so still.

He found the bus driver kneeling by his side. He was shaking and saying over and over again: 'I couldn't avoid him. He came out suddenly. I couldn't stop. I couldn't – '

Naveed's eyes were closed and there was blood streaming from his temple. A crowd quickly gathered. They seemed to Dex to be as still as Naveed: a flock of birds gathering sombrely around one of their fallen.

'Have you called the ambulance?' said Dex unreasonably to the bus driver.

'Someone's doing it,' he sobbed. 'The poor little sod. I reckon I killed him.'

Naveed groaned and opened his eyes.

'No. You haven't,' reassured Dex. But Naveed's face was slowly turning blue. Dex took his hand and squeezed it but there was no answering response.

Then Naveed muttered something and repeated more clearly: 'I made it. I beat my own record.'

'And you're going to do it again,' whispered Dex.

'It hurts.'

'You'll be all right. An ambulance is coming. Just lie still.'

Then he saw a policeman beside him with a blanket. 'I'm just going to put this over you, son,' he said gently.

'It hurts.'

'You'll be all right.'

'Where am I going?'

'Down the hospital so they can take care of you.'

'Am I hurt bad?'

The policeman shook his head. 'You'll be right as rain. You see.'

Naveed closed his eyes again and repeated: 'It hurts.'

The policeman turned to Dex and Charles and the bus driver. 'I just want to keep him warm till they get here.'

'Sure.'

'I saw you coming into the station,' the policeman said to Dex.

Dex shook his head. 'I was, but I'm going down to the hospital with him now.'

'Mate of yours?'

'I help train him. Athletics.'

'At school?'

'Yeah.'

'O.K. Here it comes.' The shrilling siren rent the sounds of the streets and the ambulance pulled up alongside the bus. The crew hurried out with a stretcher and knelt beside Naveed while the others moved back.

'He's bad,' said the copper.

The ambulance man felt Naveed's pulse.

'I think he's gone,' he said quietly.

'No,' said Dex. 'He can't be dead. He *can't* be.'

Charles put a restraining hand on his arm while the other ambulance man bent over Naveed with his head to his chest.

'I'm going to give him cardiac massage,' he said abruptly and began to press down on Naveed's chest so hard that Dex was afraid. He bumped him hard three or four times and then sat back.

Suddenly Naveed began to breathe very jerkily. The other ambulance man put an oxygen mask on his face and gradually the breathing became easier.

'Let's go,' he said. Gently they slid him on to the stretcher and carried him into the ambulance.

Dex rushed to join them. 'I'm coming,' he yelled. 'I'm his brother.'

The ambulanceman nodded and Dex jumped in the back with a vague wave at Charles. Then, with the siren screaming again, the ambulance roared into life and began to speed through the narrow congested streets.

Dex sat outside the Intensive Care Unit, waiting rest-lessly. Eventually Charles joined him.

'Any news?'

'No.'

They were sitting in a green-and-cream painted corridor and there was the familiar hospital smell of stale food and disinfectant.

'I'll sit with you.'

'Fine. But I'm not giving myself up until I know that he's O.K.'

'Right.' Charles sat down beside him, silently com-panionable. Nurses and porters passed them, giving Charles an odd look from time to time. But Dex was impervious to anything but Naveed. He looked at his watch. Just under an hour ago they had been running the Hill together. He remembered the sharing, the joy of achievement. Then Naveed had been a broken doll in the gutter. Would he ever run again?

Five minutes later Mr and Mrs Dapor and their elder son Imran joined them and Dex felt that he wanted to crawl away somewhere and hide. But, of course, none of them recognised him and they went straight into the Intensive Care Unit without so much as a backward glance. They did not emerge for another ten minutes and when they did they seemed stupified.

'What's happened?' asked Dex, unable to bear the tension any longer.

'Who are you?' Mrs Dapor stared at him without really seeing him at all.

'I train him. Sport at school.'

She nodded.

'Are you a teacher?' asked Mr Dapor, as woodenly as his wife.

'I'm in the fifth year. Please tell me how he is.'

'He's in a coma.'

'Will he come out of it? Will he recover?' Dex looked quite frantic with worry.

'He's very ill,' said Mr Dapor flatly. 'We don't know what's going to happen.'

Imran made his parents sit down and then went in search of tea. The Dapors began to pray, and the very simplicity of their prayers deeply moved Dex and in a way gave him hope. Charles, who had been sitting there with his chin buried in his dirty coat, glanced down the corridor.

'The police are here,' he said.

The policeman walked down the corridor towards them and Mr Dapor said: 'Have you come about my son? He is in the Intensive Care Unit.'

'I'm very sorry to hear that, sir.' The policeman was quite old and rather avuncular looking. 'No, I haven't come about him.' He turned to Dex. 'Are you Dexter Lloyd Warren?'

'Yeah.'

The policeman looked at the Dapors. 'Could you step down the corridor with me?'

'I'm not going anywhere. I want to see how my mate is.'

'I do understand that, but I would like a word. Would you step down the corridor with me for a moment?'

'No way.'

Charles tried to intervene. 'Dexter, I think it would be better if you went with the officer. I will come with you.'

'I'm not going anywhere.'

'This is very difficult,' said the policeman, looking at the Dapors who were still praying and did not seem to have heard anything.

Just at that moment Imran returned with paper cups full of slopping grey tea. 'What's up?'

The policeman cleared his throat. 'Is this young man known to you?'

'No.'

'I don't want to interrupt the lady and gentleman but I have to arrest this young man.'

'Well, don't do it here. We have trouble enough,' said Imran sharply.

'That's why I am asking him to accompany me down the corridor,' replied the policeman defensively. 'But he refuses to come,' he added.

Imran gently gave the tea to his father who took the cups and put them on the ground and resumed praying. Then Imran came and stood over Dex.

'Look, I don't know who you are or what you want here – '

'I'm your brother's friend. I train him in athletics. I saw the accident. He was running across the road to me when the bus hit him and I must know how he is.'

'I'm sorry but you must go with the copper before

my parents notice what's happening and get even more upset. Just go.'

'No.'

'Don't cause a scene,' said Imran in a voice of steel. He was clenching his fist.

'Please come with me, sir,' said the policeman and slowly Dex rose to his feet.

'I'm coming,' he said. Suddenly he knew that there was no alternative.

'I shall accompany him,' said Charles, getting up slowly and wheezing slightly.

'Who are you, sir?' asked the policeman irritably.

'I'm a Rasta. He's my brother.'

'You mean – ? Oh, very well, you come too. But don't cause any trouble.'

Dex turned to Imran. 'Please let me know how he is.'

Imran nodded. 'Where can I contact you?' He was prepared to be helpful now.

'Brixton police station,' said Dex sadly. '*Please* let me know.' He turned to Mrs Dapor and took her arm. 'God bless you,' he said and she smiled vaguely up at him.

Leroy phoned Gallica later that evening and once again she found that she almost resented the call.

'The boy that planted the two hundred quid on Mick has given himself up and confessed to everything – but they're still not dropping the charge against Mick.' She gave him the news flatly, without warmth or emotion.

74

'Why not?' asked Leroy, assuming she was very shocked.

'I don't know. The Newbys are going potty. I suppose they're still investigating the case and Mick's still under suspicion. Apparently they think some mates of Mick's have been on to this kid and forced him to make the confession. But something much worse has happened.'

'What now?'

'Mr Dapor's little boy Naveed. He's been knocked down and he's in a coma. It's awful, isn't it? I'm going round to see the Dapors now.'

'I thought you were coming out with me,' said Leroy.

'We'll have to fix that later in the week.'

'Can't you phone them?' Leroy knew that he was being selfish but he pressed on all the same. He didn't want to sound callous but Gallica seemed to be taking on all the troubles at Starling Point single-handed and suddenly he felt very isolated.

'This is Starling Point,' she said sharply.

'Eh?'

'You've been away a long time, Leroy. You've forgotten what it's like.'

'I remember what it was like,' he snapped. 'That's why I moved away.'

'We're a community here. We're close and if things go wrong we *see* people, not phone them.' Suddenly she was very angry and Leroy felt he was light years away from her.

'I didn't mean to be rotten about Naveed,' he said. 'I just want to see you. But I do understand. Really.'

'I don't think you do,' Gallica replied coldly and hung up on him, knowing that the second phase of their friendship was over and there would not be a third. But however much she cared about Naveed's plight it was not he who had come between them. It was the Rasta boy.

Nine

When Gallica knocked at the door of the Dapors' flat Imran answered. Sharon was there too, poking her head out of the sitting-room door.

'I just came to see how Naveed was. Mick would have come too but – ' Her voice tailed away, not knowing how to say that he couldn't face seeing Mr Dapor.

Imran looked stricken and didn't answer immediately.

'There's no change,' said Sharon.

'Am I intruding?' asked Gallica fearfully.

'Not at all.' Sharon's voice was warm. 'We're just off down to the hospital. Do you want to come?'

'I would like to but – '

She glanced at Imran and he said abruptly: 'Yes, of course. Come. We have been told to talk to him.'

'But he's – '

'Yes,' said Sharon. 'He's in a coma, but we have to try and pull him out of it. The doctor says that if we keep talking and playing tapes and asking him about his life then he might respond. They've given him a scan and they don't think there's any brain damage. But the longer he's in this coma – ' Her voice broke.

'He might turn out a vegetable,' said Imran. 'That's what he might be. A bloody vegetable.'

By eight that evening Dex had been charged and his possessions taken from him. He had signed a statement and was coming up Monday morning in the magistrates' court. Dex had been questioned for over two hours before he signed his statement, and although he knew that his mother was prepared to put up bail, he knew the police were sure that he would run and would oppose it. They seemed to believe that he had been leaned on by friends of Mick Newby's, and whatever he said could not shake them of that conviction. The more he told them that he was a lone operator, the more they told him that he wasn't. It was almost as if they were desperate to keep Mick a central figure in the case. He had asked to see his mother and the C.I.D. officer had dutifully telephoned her – but, as usual, she was not there. Dex had been bundled into a cell, given some ham sandwiches and a very unpleasant cup of milky tea and told to get some sleep. But of course he couldn't.

They had relayed news from the hospital only once, saying that there was no change in Naveed's condition and that he was 'as comfortable as could be expected' and that was all he could get out of anyone. Dex lay on his bed and thought out the dramatic events of the long day, but most of the time he relived the minutes when he and Naveed had plunged up the shifting sand and gravel of the Hill together and raced neck and neck to the top.

But the image was always followed by the sight of Naveed running across the road towards him. Dex saw the bus coming again and again and the brakes were a perpetual shriek in his mind. He saw Naveed bouncing off the bus and crashing his head with such dreadful finality on the side of the pavement. The image stayed in his mind and prevented him from sleeping for hours, and when eventually he did suddenly drop off to sleep he had an appalling nightmare when the scene was replayed time and time again. Then the nightmare changed and he found himself wandering on the Hill. The top had turned into a vast and icy mountain range. There was no snow but a kind of cold cotton-wool atmosphere. Then he saw a fellow wanderer and rushed towards him in frustrating slow motion, his feet sinking into the sponge-like surface. It was Naveed and he was mindless. His tongue protruded from his mouth and he gibbered at Dex while the saliva ran down his chin. His mouth blubbered again and in a muffled soft voice Naveed said: 'Go for it.' Then the human form dropped away and Naveed became a soft white slug. It slithered towards Dex and began to wrap itself round his legs. He screamed and screamed again and then woke in the dark cell with a policeman shining a torch in his face. Slowly Dex reorientated. The copper was young and there was kindness in his eyes.

'Bad dream, son?'

'Yeah.'

'Want a cup of tea?'

'That would be good.'

'I make it strong and sweet. That all right for you?'

'Sure.'

A few minutes later Dex was sitting on the side of his bed sipping the tea which was very comforting and just as strong and sweet as he had been promised.

'What were you dreaming about?'

'Mate of mine got knocked down yesterday. I saw it.'

'That what you're in for? Any connection?'

Dex shook his head and told him the whole story. The policeman was sympathetic.

'You're a right loon, aren't you? Fancy doing all that to get to Africa.'

'The C.I.D. keep saying Mick's mates have threatened me. I don't even know his mates. Can't you tell them it's not true? Mick had nothing to do with it.'

'I'm only a trainee round here – the lowest form of life. They won't listen to me.'

There was silence between them but it was a companionable one. Then the policeman said: 'The name's Peter.'

'Dex.'

They shook hands suddenly and rather self-consciously.

'It fascinates me.'

'What does?' asked Dex suspiciously.

'This Rasta business. Don't you smoke grass all the time?'

'I'm not telling you nothing,' said Dex quickly,

suddenly wondering if the copper had been sent in to soften him up.

'And you lot believe that Africa is your home?'

'Sure.'

'And you stole all that money and took all those risks to get there?'

'There's lots of us who would,' said Dex, his suspicion subsiding slightly.

'Steal the money?'

'Want to go back there.'

'How do you make it all out, then? How do you make out you belong in Africa?'

Dex took a long sip of his tea and told him. 'We believe that Haile Selassie, the Ethiopian emperor, was divine and that Africa must be the home for the black race. I mean the Jews got Israel, didn't they? And they pushed out the Palestinians. Or they got pushed out by someone. Most of the people in Africa are black anyway, so why shouldn't it be the natural homeland for all blacks? Why not?'

'All seems a bit far-fetched to me,' said Peter, shaking his head.

'That's because you ain't black.'

'Maybe it is.'

There was a long silence between them again. Then Dex said: 'Could you do me a favour?'

'Depends.'

'Phone the hospital and find out how that kid is.'

'All right. What's his name?'

'Naveed Dapor.'

'They know the hospital on the desk?'

'Yeah.'

'I'm on my way.'

'Thanks.'

Peter was gone for what seemed an unbearable length of time, and when he returned Dex was beside himself with anxiety.

'Well?'

'No change.'

'You mean –'

'The kid's still in a coma. They say he's as comfortable as can be expected.'

'That's all they ever say,' said Dex. 'Suppose he dies?' He looked away, his eyes full of tears.

'Want some more tea?'

'Don't go away. Don't leave me.'

Peter looked over his shoulder and Dex said: 'I suppose you have to be getting back.'

'I think I can persuade the sergeant. He's a kind bloke.'

'Persuade him to do what?'

'That we should have a game of cards and some more tea.'

Gallica had joined the Dapors and Sharon in an all-night vigil around Naveed's bedside. He still showed no sign at all of returning to consciousness, and although he gave the occasional moan he seemed in a world beyond them. Mr and Mrs Dapor prayed constantly and the Imam came several times. Imran and Sharon and Gallica took it in turns to talk to

Naveed about his hobbies, school and home life. But he showed no response whatsoever.

Towards dawn the doctor arrived. He was young and exhausted and Gallica wondered how many hours he had already worked and how many hours more he had to do.

'Has he reacted at all?'

'No,' said Mr Dapor. 'Apart from an occasional groan he has been quite still.'

The doctor nodded. 'I have to tell you that unless something dramatic happens in the next twenty-four hours he may remain in this coma for some time.'

'Could it be forever?' asked Mr Dapor and his wife began to weep silently. Sharon put her arms round her, trying to comfort her.

'It won't be forever,' the doctor said.

'What is the situation?' asked Mr Dapor.

'The longer he stays in the coma the less chance he has. If he can be stimulated though – but I know you're trying.'

'We've tried *everything*,' said Imran hopelessly. 'We've talked for hours about football and sport and friends and even Pakistan. We've talked about the mosque and the Imam has been here trying to talk to him as well. We've talked about the sprint he's been training for. Everything.'

'Hang on,' said Gallica. 'What abut Dex?'

'Who's Dex?' asked the doctor.

'At Naveed's school there's a lot of trouble with truanting and fights and all that and the headmaster decided to set up a challenge. He built a kind of hill in the school grounds made of sand and gravel. It's quite high and you have to race up it and there's a champion each term who can do the climb in the fastest time. Naveed's being trained by this guy Dex – ' Gallica's voice died away. She turned to Imran and Sharon. 'You thinking what I'm thinking?' She turned back to the bewildered doctor. 'Dex is someone Naveed hero-worships – a fifth year at Starling Point. He's a brilliant athlete and he's been training him to run the Hill and Naveed's been getting better and better timings. Then Dex got into trouble with the police and was arrested today. That's how the accident happened. Naveed was running across the road to Dex as he was going in the police station.'

'So he's in custody?'

'As far as we know,' said Gallica.

'It doesn't sound as if the police are likely to release him,' said the doctor. 'Are they?'

But now it was Mrs Dapor who spoke and they turned to her, surprised that she had been listening so carefully.

'If this Dex is brought here, do you think he could help my son?' she asked the doctor.

'Any immediate memory will help. Anything his mind was really caught up with would have a chance,' he said very positively.

Mrs Dapor rose to her feet quickly.

'Where are you going?' asked her husband.

'I am going to the police station,' she said. 'Will you come with me?'

Ten

The small Pakistani lady was immediately rebuffed.

'But my son is in a coma. This Dex is the only person in the world who can help him.'

'Warren has been charged and is waiting a court appearance in the morning. There is no question of him being released. I'm sorry,' said the kind but unimaginative desk sergeant who always stuck to the rules come what may.

'Then I must speak to someone in higher authority,' she said forcefully.

Mr Dapor knew he must not interfere. His wife was the most determined person he knew, and once she believed in something she'd never leave it alone. So he watched and waited, seeing the desk sergeant becoming angry.

'There's no point in going over my head, madam. I can assure you of that.'

'There is every point. It is a matter of life and death for my son.' Her voice was steady. Mr Dapor looked at his watch. It was just after six in the morning.

'I'm afraid there's nothing more I can do,' the desk sergeant said abruptly.

'But you must. And if you don't, I shall search this police station for a person of higher authority.'

'I am going to ask you to leave.'

'Then you will have to carry me bodily from this place.'

The desk sergeant stared at her angrily. Then he said: 'I'll ring the C.I.D. They will probably have you forcibly removed.'

He rang from the back of the office so she could not hear what he was saying and about five minutes later a middle-aged man appeared.

'Mrs Dapor?'

'Yes.'

'Can you explain this situation to me, please?' said the C.I.D. man with tolerant weariness.

'My son is in a coma and this Dex – he is close to my son – he can talk to him. And if he can strike a chord then the doctor says my son will live.'

'And what makes you think he will strike a chord?'

'There is a competition in the school. Something about running up an artificial hill in the school grounds. It is a great ambition for my son to win this and this Dex has been helping him. Training him.'

Suddenly the C.I.D. man seemed interested. 'I know the hill. There's been some police training on it and we're offering a prize. I think it's a damn good idea. What do you want me to do? Bring the prisoner to the hospital?'

'Please.' She stared at him, hardly able to believe her good fortune.

'For how long?'

'I can't tell you that.'

'It would mean putting back his court appearance. But I think in the circumstances the court might understand. We will obviously have to send an escort with him, and that escort will have to remain with him at all times.'

'I understand that.'

The desk sergeant was staring at the C.I.D. man pop-eyed. Mr Dapor smiled at his wife. He always thought highly of her but he had never felt so proud as he did on this particular early morning.

'When do you want him?'

'Now. Every moment counts.'

'I'll have him woken up.' He hurried away, leaving the Dapors with a tiny spark of hope glowing in their hearts.

Peter woke Dex up a few minutes later.

'Dex.'

'Mm.'

'Wake up.'

Dex woke from a confused flurry of bad dreams. 'What do you want?'

'That kid Naveed.'

'He's dead?' He sat bolt upright and began to shake from head to foot. 'He's dead, isn't he?'

'No. He wants you. Or at least his parents do.'

'You mean he's woken up?'

'No. But they think that if you talk to him hard enough it might help.'

'I can go to the hospital?'

'Under escort.'

'Blimey. What about the court?'

'That's going to be postponed.'

'Who's taking me?'

Peter gave him a self-conscious smile. 'Me. And they're not happy about that, either. But they can't spare anyone from the C.I.D. I suppose they think I'm too green for villains like you.'

'I won't give you no trouble.'

'I can take your word on that, can I?'

'Yeah.'

'They're going to drive us down the hospital and then pick us up again.'

'When?'

'Whenever.'

Despite all the precautions Dex felt heady with delight. At last he had the chance that he never thought he would get. Could he save Naveed? In the back of his mind he knew that it was a far-fetched hope, but he wanted to cling on to it more than anything else in the world.

When Dex arrived at the hospital with Peter his heart sank. The room seemed crowded with people and he suddenly felt acutely self-conscious. And when he looked at Naveed, he seemed to have already slipped away to some remote place from which he could never be recovered. Then he saw the black girl that he had rescued and his hopes rose. Everyone else looked hostile and suspicious except her – and the Pakistani lady who came up to him and took his hand gently. She was very small and delicate and there was a look of hope in her eyes that was painful to see.

'You are Dex?'

He could see all the others looking doubtfully at his dreadlocks and dirty tousled clothes.

'Yeah.'

'And you know my son?'

'Very well.'

'Can you talk to him about your Hill?'

'You bet.' Dex went across to the bed and sat down beside Naveed.

'Can I take his hand?' he asked and Mrs Dapor nodded.

'Well Mick?'

It was nine a.m. in the police station and D.I. Cook had asked Mick to come back to the station. He looked in a bad way, exhausted and hopeless.

'You won't be going to court this morning,' said the D.I.

'Why not?'

'Because they've decided to take your mate on some errand of mercy. Something about a kid in a coma.'

Mick nodded, hardly listening to him. 'I dunno why you're keeping on at me, when he's said he did it and all,' he began.

'But we don't believe him, son.'

'I don't have the kind of mates you're talking about. I don't know anyone who leans on people.'

'You had a gang of mates who attacked the round-about owner a couple of years back.'

'Someone else put them up to it. Not me.'

'And you've just finished probation and you walked out of your job?'

'Dapor accused me of taking some money.'

'Which you did.'

'We've been through all this,' said Mick desperately.

'And we're going through it again, aren't we?'

'I put the fiver back.'

'But you took it in the first place.'

'Yeah.'

'You stole it?'

'I borrowed it.'

'So how do you expect us to believe that you didn't steal the two hundred?'

'Because the black guy with the dreadlocks stole it. He took it when I was in the stock room.'

'Sure he did. Is that why you had two hundred quid on you when you were arrested?'

'He planted it on me. He told you. I've told you – dozens of times.'

'He could have confessed under duress.'

'No one threatened him.'

'A kid like that wouldn't make a confession unless he was well under pressure.'

'Why?'

'Because he's tough. He's a Rasta, isn't he?'

'That doesn't mean he's tough.'

'Come on, Mick.'

'Come on what?'

'Be straight with me. It's your only chance. It's going to go much better in court for you if you admit the truth.'

'I am admitting the truth.' The conversation was becoming a battleground and Mick was beginning to feel so exhausted that he was worried he could be tripped up any moment.

'You were partners, weren't you? Partners on this thieving?'

'Would I do my own house?'

'Yes. To throw us off the scent. And you have to admit that there's not a lot of love lost between you and your parents, is there?'

'What do you mean?'

'Your dad says there isn't.'

'He would. I love my sister. Do you think I'd give her a shock like that?'

'If it was to get back at your parents.'

'No.'

'Come on, Mick. Tell me the truth. It'll go so much easier for you if you do.'

'I *have* told you the truth!'

For a moment, Mick felt like caving in and telling him what he wanted to hear. Then he stopped himself. He wouldn't drop himself in it. He was determined he wouldn't.

'Mick. You and Dex were partners,' Cook continued relentlessly. 'You may have fallen out now but you were partners all right. Tell me the truth and then it's going to be – '

'Yeah, I know. So much easier for me. But what you're saying is a lie. Get it?'

'The D.I. sighed. 'I'll give you another few hours to think it over.'

'I don't need another few hours.'

'You stay here and think it over.'

'My answer will be the same – and I want to go home.'

'You'll go home when we're ready,' said D.I. Cook angrily.

Gallica listened to Dex talking to Naveed as if there was nothing else in the world but his voice. She found him riveting and he made her feel as if she was climbing the Hill as well. He began slowly, almost hesitantly, but then he very quickly warmed up.

'You see, Naveed, you have to feel that Hill in your soul like I could feel Africa. You have to know the Hill and understand it and not be afraid of it. You still don't know how hard it can be, like I don't know how hard Africa can be, but we both know that we're gonna get there. We're gonna run that Hill together and we're going to feel that shifting sand and the hardness of that gravel and, man, we're gonna fly. We're going up side by side, and we're not gonna stop until we reach the top and then we're gonna shout and rave and break every record in the damned book.

'On the way up it's like we're brothers. Like we're one. One body with double the energy right, man? We're flying. We're leaving the others behind. We're going to conquer that sand and gravel and nothing's going to defeat us this time, man. But you have to wake up because you have to get training again; you can't lie there and take it easy no more. Are you getting the message? You can't lie there. You have to run the Hill. And you have to run it with me, man. And what are we running it for? We're running it for Africa, and I just had this great idea. You want to know what it is? Well, I want you to get well because you have to help me. I lost sight of my homeland and I've got myself in trouble, right? Well, I'm gonna tell that judge – plead with that judge – that he needs to put me on probation because I have to run that Hill for Africa, not for some damn charity but for the Rastas.

'But I ain't got no fellow Rastas to run with. I only got you, and I want you, Naveed. You have to help me, Naveed. I been helping you, haven't I? Well, you got to help me now. Get up out of that bed and help me, man, because it's a good story to tell the judge and it's a true one. But if you don't damned well wake up I'm going down – and that's going to be the end of me. I can't live in prison. I can't have my freedom taken away. Not just like that. You have to help me. You have to wake up.' Dex paused exhausted, and there was complete silence in the room. He looked down at Naveed, but there was not the slightest change in him at all.

Dex tried to reach Naveed throughout the rest of the morning, and the more Gallica watched and listened to him the more she seemed to absorb his single-minded passion. She knew the others were impressed, but it was more to her than that. She was captivated. She was also frantic with worry, wondering how long they would allow him to stay here. The nice but nervous-looking young policeman might take him back to the police station at any time.

When they were drinking tea and Dex was having a much-needed rest, she asked the policeman surreptitiously: 'How long can he stay?'

'He's not making a lot of progress, miss,' said Peter slowly.

'Please let him stay.'

'Question is how long will it take? I don't think they'll wear any longer than late afternoon.'

'Ring them. Ask if he can stay – at least for twenty-four hours.'

But Mrs Dapor had overheard them and she said: 'Don't worry. I shall phone them myself.'

She walked out of the room abruptly, leaving everyone in a state of high tension. When she returned ten minutes later she looked triumphant.

'I have got the extension until seven tomorrow morning. And that was all they were prepared to allow.'

'It's got to be enough,' said Dex, his hand shaking on the tea cup. 'It's just got to be.'

Mick lay on his bed and thought hard about his life. If only he hadn't taken that fiver. That was why no one trusted him. That and the past. Now they were prepared to lay practically anything on him. It was bloody unfair but he could see why right enough. And what the hell was he going to do to prove that he wasn't leaning on Dex? That he hadn't been associated with him?

Half an hour later Mick was told that his sister had come to see him and that he could have ten minutes with her in the presence of a policeman.

Sharon looked wan and tired when Mick arrived in the interview room, and when she explained to him what had been happening at the hospital he was torn between sorrow for the Dapors and a deep sense of self-pity. Self-pity understandably won.

'I'm sorry about the kid. Really I am. But who the hell's going to do anything about me? No one seems to believe a word I say and the police are really hassling me. I feel trapped, Sharon. In the end they'll just convict me for something I honestly didn't do.'

'We've got to get Dex to really *prove* he's not being leant on,' said Sharon. 'And I can think of a way of doing it.'

'How?'

'Gallica.'

'Her? What connection has she got with him?'

'I think she fancies him.'

'Of all people! What about Leroy?'

'I don't know. But I *do* know her. I can see it in her eyes.'

'All because he helped her that time?'

'No, it's more than that.'

'And you reckon — what? That she can get him to really come clean?'

'I think she could get him to really lay it down to the police – to close up any loopholes.'

'They've got it in for me anyway,' said Mick miserably. 'My past is catching up with me.'

'You sound like a gangster.' Sharon suddenly giggled.

'It's not funny.'

'I know. But I'm sure she can help.'

'Fancy her falling for grot like that,' Mick snapped sourly.

'You might be pleased she has,' replied Sharon.

Throughout the afternoon and early evening Naveed lay still, only emitting a slight groan from time to time. Dex spent all his time sitting beside him, holding his hand or talking, talking about the Hill. He hardly paused, except for occasional breaks for drinks and the food that he found so hard to swallow. Slowly a feeling of desperation was overcoming him and the Dapors, Gallica, Imran and Sharon seemed to grow more and more depressed.

Finally at seven, Mr Dapor insisted that his wife took a rest next door and Imran said: 'Let's leave Dex alone with Naveed. At least – ' he glanced in the direction of Peter – 'almost alone.'

'Can't I stay?' asked Gallica and Dex said: 'Yeah, I'd like her to.'

'I'll go and get some tea together,' said Sharon. 'And I'll bring it in to your mum and dad and you, Imran.'

'Great.'

The door closed behind them all and Dex and Gallica were alone, except for Peter who sat quietly by the door.

'I'd better start talking again,' said Dex.

'Give yourself a bit of a rest.'

'Five minutes, then.'

They sat beside Naveed silently, watching him breathe. That, and the occasional turning of a page of the novel Peter was reading, was the only sound in the room.

Then Dex said: 'My dream slipped away. He brought it back.'

'Naveed?'

'Yeah. It could have gone forever.'

'Africa – I can remember it all quite vividly, although we left when I was seven.'

He turned to her. 'I thought you were born here.'

'No. Actually I'm an African queen.' She laughed.

'What did you say?'

'I'm an African queen. But it's only a kind of honorary title – a tribal one, really. It doesn't mean anything.'

'It does. It means everything.'

'My uncle out there in Zimbabwe. He's quite rich. Maybe he would take you on.'

'What at?'

'He has a farm. You'd need to go to college.'

'Out there?'

'Well – you could do.'

'He wouldn't take the likes of me.'

'You don't know him. I could write.'

'As a charity case.'

'No, just as an opportunity.'

'It's no good. I'll be inside.'

'A lot of people are going to stand up for you.'

'Won't do any good.'

Suddenly Gallica reached out and took Dex's hand. 'Don't throw yourself away.'

She had never felt like this for anyone before. Not for Leroy or Mick or anyone. It was extraordinary – this beautiful boy with his dreadlocks, the awful things he had done, the crazy dreams he had. Well, he had rescued her, hadn't he? She would have been raped if he hadn't turned up. But Gallica knew it was nothing to do with that. She was just dangerously attracted to him. Suddenly she knew that she would not only wait for him but she would go anywhere with him. Just anywhere. Like Africa, for instance. But the question was – would he want her to wait for him? But at least he was returning the pressure of her hand and then, to her intense surprise, he leant over and kissed her.

'I've been thinking about you. Ever since that night.'

'You rescued me.'

'Couldn't very well leave you to it, could I?'

'Suppose I waited for you. Suppose we went to Africa together?'

'I'd be going with royalty – I'd be going with a queen.'

'Don't joke.'

'I'm not.'

'I *will* wait.'

'Really?' He looked at her doubtfully. 'I could be away a long time.'

'I'll still wait.'

'It's not fair on you.'

'I want to.'

'You don't know me.'

'I don't have to.'

'I'm a villain.'

'You're Dex. I want you so much.'

Abruptly he turned away from her, snatching back his hand and putting it into Naveed's.

'We're wasting *his* time,' said Dex. 'And if we waste it, he won't have any.'

He began his torrent of words again. Gallica sat back and listened. She had never been so in love before.

'You have to get some sleep,' said Mr Dapor to Dex.

'No.'

'It's after twelve.'

'I don't have long.' He glanced at Peter who was asleep in his chair. 'I've got to reach Naveed. Somehow.'

'Take five minutes.'

But Dex turned his back on him and, his voice hoarse, began again. 'Listen, Naveed. If you don't damn well wake up I'm gonna thump you.'

Mr Dapor smiled. Dex was rapidly winning his way into his heart. Then something happened. Naveed opened his eyes. Dex's voice stuttered to a halt and Mr Dapor rushed over to his son. Peter, as if by some joyous vibration, woke up and came to the bedside. Mrs Dapor, who had just been to make sure Imran was getting some sleep in the other room, came in and sensed something had happened.

'His eyes are open,' said Mr Dapor quietly as she walked towards him.

Gallica and Sharon were also trying to get some rest and so just the four of them stood electrified by Naveed's bedside.

'Dex?' Now he was speaking.

'Yeah?'

'What happened?'

'You got knocked down. By a bus.'

'Blimey. Am I hurt?'

'Bump on the head.'

'I been dreaming about the Hill.'

'And?'

'I dreamt I won it. You kept shouting at me.'

'You bet I did.'

'Naveed.' Mrs Dapor's eyes were streaming with tears as she knelt down beside the bed. 'Naveed.'

'Mum. What are you crying about? And Dad – you're crying too. And who's the copper?'

'Name of Peter,' he said. 'Good to see you awake.'

'How long have I been out?'

'Hours and hours,' said Dex. 'Don't we all feel it?'

'Get the doctor,' said Mrs Dapor. 'Get him now.'

Naveed's bedside was crowded with people although

he tired very easily. The doctor was delighted and he said to Dex: 'You did the trick.'

'He worked himself into the ground,' said Peter.

'I've examined him,' pronounced the doctor. 'He'll be fine – once he's recovered from severe concussion. He must have a tough skull.'

'He's pretty thick,' joked Dex.

Naveed stirred from drifting off into sleep. 'Dex – '

'What is it, mate?'

'I just remembered. Weren't you nicked for something?' Naveed's voice was drowsy and insubstantial.

'Don't worry about that. I got off, didn't I?'

'Did you?'

'Yeah. Magistrate put me on probation. Didn't he, Peter?'

'Who's Peter?'

'Copper. Mate of mine. We got friendly in the nick and he wanted to come down and see you.'

'Did he?'

'Yes,' said Peter, playing his part. 'Glad you're feeling better.'

Naveed closed his eyes again. Then he said: 'He really got off, didn't he, Peter?'

'He's going to be all right now,' he replied and Dex grinned at him, pleased by his understanding complicity.

'Got to go now, Naveed.' Dex leant over him and suddenly kissed him on the forehead. 'Be seeing you.'

'When do we run the Hill next?' Naveed murmured.

'Get out of that bed,' said Dex. 'Fast.'

Once in the corridor, Dex turned to Peter.

'Hang on.'

'Why?'

'I want a pee.' Dex was sweating and Peter looked agitated.

'I'll come with you.'

'Right. Where was it?'

'Down here somewhere.' Peter looked vaguely down the empty corridor. It was three o'clock in the morning and he felt very vulnerable.

'There it is.'

'Where?'

'Here.' Dex thumped him as hard as he could in the stomach and ran. But he had largely misplaced his punch and although it made Peter stagger, the force of the blow only connected with his belt and within seconds he was in pursuit.

Eleven

Freedom mattered more than anything else in the world to Dex at that moment. He was instinctive, and like a wild animal he was determined not to be shut up. So he pounded down the corridor with Peter a few metres behind him. Neither of them spoke; there was too much at stake to waste breath. Dex ran on, darting glances from left to right, hoping for some means of escape from his pursuer. Desperate, he banged his way through some rubber doors and sped into a long, half-lit room. A bright light suddenly snapped on and a startled nurse stared up at him as he tore down past rows of beds.

'What are you doing, young man? This is a geriatric ward. You can't come in here,' she scolded.

But Dex ran silently on.

'Officer, what's going on?' she squealed at Peter as he dashed past her.

'I'm chasing a suspect, madam,' he said without pausing.

'You can't chase one in here.'

'Sorry, we can never choose our time,' said Peter as he raced on.

'What's up?' asked an old lady.

'Settle down now, Mrs Griffin.'

'Playing cops and robbers, are we?'

'Settle down, *please*.'

The opposite rubber doors swung to on Peter as he tried to speed up.

'Well,' said old Mrs Chubb. 'It makes a difference, doesn't it? I mean it's a *novelty*.'

'Disgraceful, I call it,' said Miss Chard, sitting up in bed. 'I shall need my pan now I've been woken. Nurse. Nurse. Where is that woman? Kindly fetch a bedpan.'

'Got the runs, have you?' asked vulgar Mrs Rankle. 'That's nasty.'

Soon the ward was a cacaphony of sound and the furious night nurse was run off her feet.

'I'll complain,' she said as she hurriedly grabbed a bedpan.

'It was a bit of fun,' remonstrated Mrs Griffin. 'You don't get much fun in here.'

Keeping a few metres in front of Peter, Dex finally made the car park. At the far end he saw a small Fiesta coming towards him. He flagged it down.

'Emergency?'

'Yes.'

Dex wrenched at the passenger door and thankfully found it open. He hurled himself in, much to the consternation of the driver – an elderly midwife named Mrs Middle.

'Drive,' he said, conscious of Peter, centimetres

away, shouting out the word 'police'. But the elderly woman didn't seem to hear either of them.

'Eh?'

'I said drive. Or I'll kill you.'

'You'll what?'

'I got a gun.'

Mrs Middle put her foot down just as Peter reached the car.

'Stop! Police!' he gasped.

But she was already in third gear, shooting out of the hospital car park and leaving Peter grasping at thin air and yelling into his radio. He hadn't thought to use it until now, he'd been so sure of catching Dex. He'd be in trouble for that, he knew, as he called for assistance.

In the car, Dex leant over and said: 'I won't hurt you if you drive like the clappers.'

Mrs Middle nodded and put her foot down again. 'Where am I going?' she panted.

'Africa,' he said.

He's probably a psychiatric patient, thought Mrs Middle tremulously.

In fact they drove to Clapham Common and it was there that Dex told her to stop. He got out and ran across the common towards the South Circular Road, hearing the sirens and watching the police cars bear down on Mrs Middle's Fiesta. By now, Dex knew he didn't stand a chance. Then he saw the truck.

'So you let the master criminal escape. You're for the high jump, son. The station officer, still smarting from being overruled by the C.I.D., was only too delighted to take Peter apart – and Peter knew that it wasn't only the station officer who was going to do that. There would be hell to pay with the C.I.D.

'Look, I – '

'You haven't got a leg to stand on. And you know it.'

'Yes, sarge.'

'A kid like that – and you let him go.'

'He can run!'

'He shouldn't have been running in the first place.'

'Yes, sarge.'

'So I'm going to boil you in oil, Peter. Boil you in oil.'

Gallica arrived home exhausted at six o'clock in the morning. Her mother had just woken and was laying breakfast for her father.

'Is he –?' she began tentatively.

'He's alive. He woke. And it's all thanks to Dex. He talked and talked to him about racing up that Hill – and this morning Naveed opened his eyes and started talking. If it hadn't been for Dex, he'd still be in that coma.'

Her mother was visibly moved and she pulled Gallica gently to her and held her close.

'I'm so glad, my darling. So glad.'

'The Dapors are over the moon.'

'God bless them.'

'And the doctor said that with plenty of rest he could be out of hospital in a fortnight.'

'It's a miracle.'

'It's Dex.'

'You must sleep soon.'

'I could sleep for hours. But Dex ran for it.'

'Oh no –'

'He managed to get away from the young copper who brought him.'

'Where does that leave Mick?'

'Nowhere. Sharon had asked me to speak to Dex – try to get him to really convince the police that Mick was innocent. But I didn't get the chance.'

'You can't do everything.' Her mother released her, stroking Gallica's hair. 'You've done as much as you can.'

'Now he's done a runner.'

'There is someone who could help.'

'Help Mick? Who?'

'Suppose Mr Dapor went to see them. Really talked about how well Mick had done in the supermarket – how he'd left his past behind him.'

'Would he?'

'I'm sure he would. I'll ring him later.'

'Mum, you are terrific.' Gallica gave a huge yawn. Despite the miracle of Naveed's return to consciousness, she felt a great gnawing ache in the pit of her stomach. Dex had gone. Would she ever see him again? She just wanted to be alone now, in her bed, thinking of him. 'I'll go on up, Mum.'

'There's just one thing, Gallica.' Mrs Dumas paused hesitantly.

'Yes?'

'You have a visitor. He's in the front room.'

'Dex has given himself up?'

'What?'

'Is it Dex?'

'Why should he come here?' Mrs Dumas stared at her daughter aghast and Gallica realised that she would have to talk fast to stop her mother guessing how she felt about him.

'I'm so tired, Mum. I think I'm going potty.'

Her mother smiled and all trace of suspicion disappeared from her face.

'Shall I tell Leroy you can't see him?'

'No,' said Gallica with a sinking heart. 'Don't do that.'

'Shall I make some coffee?'

'I'll need it.' She walked heavily into the front room which was full of coloured photographs and the best furniture and was never used except for the most formal of occasions – one of which seemed to be Leroy's visit. He was sitting uncomfortably on the edge of a chair with a plastic cover and jumped up when she came in.

'Are you all right?'

'Sure.' They brushed lips and she sat down wearily on the hard sofa and quickly brought Leroy up to date.

'And don't say it's all like a soap opera,' she concluded.

'I wasn't going to. I was going to say how I miss Starling Point.' He looked her straight in the eyes. 'You've met someone, haven't you?'

'I don't know what you mean.'

'Yes, you do. It was the tone of your voice on the phone.'

'I was worried.'

'Gallica, please tell me the truth.'

She paused, swallowed and then said guiltily: 'There is someone.'

'I thought so.' He looked curiously relieved.

'Do you mind – very badly?'

'I took off last time. Now it's your turn.' His voice was neutral and there was no trace of bitterness in it.

'That doesn't answer the question.'

'I love you, Gallica. I always will. But it's not going to work out, however hard we try. I belong to the fairground; you belong to Starling Point. And they don't belong together.'

'We shouldn't let places – jobs – come between us.'

'They do. You were right. I don't belong here any longer. I sometimes want to but it's too late now. Jim's offered me a partnership and I'm really happy with the Gallopers.'

'Did you come here to tell me all this?'

'Yeah. Your mum put me up for the night. She's a nice lady.'

'So – have you got anyone?'

'Travelling about like we do?' He grinned. 'I'd be lucky. I'll meet someone – don't worry.'

'I *do* worry.'

'Don't. I'm happy. Can I ask you – who this guy is? This lucky guy.'

'I can't say. Mum would be livid.'

'I hope I don't guess right.'

'Maybe you do. But he's on the run now and I probably won't see him again, ever.'

'You don't want to see him again,' said Leroy firmly. 'The guy's trouble. Bad trouble.'

'I love him,' she said hopelessly.

Leroy came across and kissed her on the cheek. 'That's a friendly kiss,' he said.

'I know.'

'I don't want to tell you how to run your life. I'm just afraid for you, that's all. I don't want you hurt.'

'He wouldn't hurt me.'

'I'm not talking about the physical.' He looked at his watch. 'I must get back.'

'Don't you want any breakfast?'

'Haven't got time.'

'Leroy – '

'Yes?'

'We will always be friends, won't we?'

'I want to be.'

'I shall be needing you.'

'You only have to call.'

They walked out of the stuffy front room and into the hall where he kissed her once again.

'Be seeing you.'

She watched him walk out of the estate. He waved and she blew him a kiss. Then Gallica staggered up to bed and just before she drifted off to sleep Mrs Dumas brought some coffee in.

'I didn't want to interrupt you, and he'd already had some.'

'Thanks, Mum. I just want to sleep now.'

'O.K. But Gallica – is everything all right between you and Leroy?'

'It couldn't be better, Mum. It just couldn't be better.'

'I'm so glad. Sleep well.'

Gallica fell asleep almost immediately and dreamt of Dex. They were making love on an African veldt. There was the particular smell of Africa that she still remembered from a child and could not get out of her nostrils. When they had finished making love, they walked down to a pool which was still and cooling in the lessening heat of the evening sun. They swam – and kissed – and made love again on the sandy shore. Dusk came and they looked up to the red orb of the setting sun. Then, on the way back to the village, she lost him in the dark.

Twelve

True to her word, Mrs Dumas called Mr Dapor at about nine at the hospital.

'How is he?'

'Eating breakfast.' She could hear the smile in his voice.

'I'm so glad.'

'Of course, he is still very weak.'

'That's natural.'

'But the doctors are very pleased with him. We have a lot to thank young Dex for – but unfortunately he did a bunk, as they say. That will ensure things go very badly for him indeed.'

'Is there – does anybody know where he is?'

'They've asked Charles – the old recluse and his girlfriend who live in the squat. But they say they've no idea.'

'He leaves a problem.'

'I was going to deal with that.'

'You mean Mick?'

'The police have been giving him a bad time. But I was going to go up to the police station and talk to them.'

'You're a good man.'

'No, I'm an average man. But I've lived in Starling Point long enough to know that people need a chance. And Michael – as he has always wanted to be known and never quite has been – Michael has a good track record with me. They should know it.'

'You're still a good man,' she said.

'Inspector Cook, please.'

'I'll see if he's in.'

Mr Dapor looked round the interior of the police station nervously, wondering if he could pull the interview off. He didn't have his wife's confidence in outside places like this and he dreaded the hard-edged interview he was going to have. Eventually D.I. Cook arrived, young, aggressive with a trim little moustache and a fashionable suit. Mr Dapor felt worse directly he saw him.

Without saying much, Cook ushered him into a small, claustrophobic interview room and sat down opposite him at a small rickety table that was stained with tea-cup rings. Not that he offered him any tea. The air smelt of stale cigarettes.

'Well, Mr Dapor, you wanted to talk to me about young Mick?' Cook sounded brisk and hearty – a combination Mr Dapor did not like.

'I have come to tell you that, although he made a silly mistake with the five pounds, I am sure he did not steal the two hundred, nor was he mixed up in anything with that boy Dex.'

'You can give us some evidence to support that?'

'No. But I am sure.'

'That's not evidence, Mr Dapor.'

'Do you have any?' He was gaining a little more confidence now.

'I'm afraid I can't divulge that.'

'He is a good boy. I wouldn't have him as a trainee manager if I thought he was really dishonest. Michael has worked for me for almost two years now and I am very pleased with him. In fact I am so pleased that I am going to give him the position of manager of a small new branch I am opening in Sunderland Street.'

'Are you?' Suddenly Cook seemed impressed. '*Him* – a manager? With his record?'

'It's not that bad.'

'It's not good. And with Warren on the run –'

He paused, losing a little of his briskness. 'We caught Newby with two hundred pounds in stolen bank notes on him. Your stolen bank notes. He has got himself a solicitor – or rather his father has. It's not me you've got to convince. It's the magistrate.'

Mr Dapor stared at him, feeling horribly naive. He had come to the wrong man – at the wrong time.

'I'm sorry.'

But D.I. Cook seemed to soften. 'We're bringing the charges against him, you see. But if you speak to Mr Newby I'm sure his solicitor would want you in as a character witness. Off the record, I reckon you'd make a damn good one. He's a very lucky lad to have someone like you to stick up for him – someone to back him.'

'I only speak as I find.'

'Mr Dapor – '

'Yes?'

'Would you like a cup of tea?'

Gallica spent most of the next day sitting with Naveed who was now talking, eating – and sleeping. She had pleaded not to have to go to school – as had Sharon – and Gallica was glad that she was distracted by the joy of Naveed's recovery – and able to have periods of contemplation about Dex when Naveed was asleep. At one point she was alone with Sharon.

'Where do you think he is now?' asked Gallica.

'Hitching. But I've got something to tell you that might help.'

'What?' Gallica was desperate to know.

'I would have told you before but while Naveed was awake I didn't want to. I thought it might upset him.'

'Yes?' Gallica was almost unable to bear the strain of waiting.

'I saw that dirty-looking old tramp Charles – and he told me Dex gave him two thousand pounds to give to the police. And he did.'

'Are you sure?'

'I don't think he would have told me if he hadn't.'

'Thank God.'

'It should go towards – what do they call it? – mitigating circumstances.'

'Maybe.'

'You're going through it, aren't you?'

'Yes. I think about him all the time.'

'Leroy?'

'We've both accepted that we're just going to be friends.'

'So you're serious about Dex?'

'Like no one else.'

'He's a villain.'

'Not if he gives himself up.' said Gallica rather unconvincingly.

'But will he?'

'He wants to go to Africa.'

'He won't get there hitching. Hang on,' Sharon saw something in Gallica's eyes. 'You mean – '

'I'm his African queen,' said Gallica. She laughed and then began to cry. Blinking back her tears, she said: 'Well, we *could* go together.'

'Of course you could,' said Sharon reluctantly.

'You trying to humour me?'

'No.'

'You think it's a crazy scheme?'

'For you, no. You've got your uncle. But for him – I don't think he could sustain it. He's full of dreams.'

'Maybe.'

'And Gallica – '

'Mm?'

'I bet you'll be angry. But don't think you can reform him, either.'

'Gallica smiled sadly. 'I did have that in mind.'

'Mr Dapor, you have something to tell us about Michael?'

The magistrate was a middle-aged man with glasses and a sympathetic manner. Mr Dapor wondered if he owned a shop.

'Yes, Michael worked for me as a managerial trainee in my supermarket. I have employed him for the last eighteen months and I am very satisfied with his honesty, his application, hard work and self-discipline. In fact, I have been so satisfied that I am putting him in as manager in my new shop in Sunderland Street. I do accept he made a stupid mistake in borrowing a fiver from the till, but not that he stole the two hundred pounds which I am sure was planted on him in some way or other. I would ask the court to show him leniency so that he can continue with his work.' He finished his carefully rehearsed speech and then stared up beseechingly into the eyes of the magistrate.

'Thank you.' The magistrate turned to the two colleagues either side of him and began a session of what seemed to Mr Dapor interminable whispering. He glanced towards the chairs at the side and saw Imran, Gallica, Sharon and Mrs Dapor looking very tense while Mick, standing stiffly in front of the bench, looked desperate. Sitting by themselves, a little distance away from the others, Mr and Mrs Newby had created their own little island of outraged respectability.

At last the magistrate turned back. 'Mr Dapor, we are most grateful for your comments and Michael is most fortunate in having you as his employer. But you must appreciate that he has only recently come off probation.' There was a grisly silence and Sharon could see the sweat pouring off her brother's forehead. Then the magistrate continued. 'However, his probation report is good.' He turned to Mick. 'The trouble is, Michael, that we still have no explanation of how you came by the two hundred – '

'It was planted,' said Mick.

'Don't interrupt,' said the magistrate brusquely. 'As I was saying – the two hundred pounds and, as Mr Warren has absconded, the police are unable to pursue their enquiries until he is arrested. But in the light of your good work record I am going to release you – ' There was a stifled cheer from Mick's supporters and the magistrate frowned – 'until such time as the police are able to pursue their enquiries again when Mr Warren is hopefully apprehended. Do you understand?'

'Yes, sir,' said Mick, trying to look both humble, grateful and angelic at the same time and rather failing in all three.

'And you do appreciate you have a generous and supportive employer?'

'He's terrific,' said Mick. And this time he could not have looked more genuine.

Thirteen

September.

Gallica had gradually become despondent about Dex. Despite the passing of time, she still missed him desperately but there had been no trace of his whereabouts whatsoever. Meanwhile Naveed had made a complete recovery. He had been training hard for the Hill again and the competition was to be held the following afternoon.

Tonight Gallica slept restlessly, dreaming of Africa and Dex. It was the old, familiar, much-loved dream: the water hole, the swimming, the love-making, the veldt. But in fact by now Gallica had given him up and her parents were worried for she was apathetic and anti-social. Sharon insisted on visiting regularly, but for the most part she had sunk into a fantasy life, punctuated with speculations about Dex.

At about three she suddenly found she was wide awake and wondered what had woken her. But when she went to the kitchen for a glass of water she heard a sharp sound. Someone was tapping on the window so softly it was barely recognisable. Fearfully she pressed her nose to the window pane which looked into a side alley between the blocks. There was a shadow crouched there and she was about to scream when, with a considerable shock, Gallica realised who it was.

'Shh.'

Gallica opened the kitchen door and Dex came in. He was filthy, with matted dreadlocks and had lost at least a stone. Gallica stared at him, unable to speak, unable to believe he had come back at last. He was literally like someone out of a dream.

'Got any food?'

She continued to stare.

'Did someone cut your tongue out?'

Gallica went to the larder and gave him some bread and cheese. He wolfed it down and she gave him more. As he ate, she found her voice again.

'Where have you been?'

'Sleeping rough.'

'For so long?'

'Yeah. I been all over the place. Scotland, the North. Birmingham.'

'Did you get work?'

'Casual.'

'Been in trouble?'

'Nothing to speak of.'

'Why –?'

'Am I back? I couldn't take no more of it. I stuck it out long enough.' He grinned. 'Didn't get to Africa. Only Glasgow.'

'What are you going to do now?'

'Depends on you?'

'I don't get it.'

'You should. Will you still wait for me?'

She crossed over to the table and put her hands on his thin shoulders. 'I've thought of nothing else *but* you.'

'That's amazing – all this time?'

'All this time.'

'I've come back to turn myself in to the Old Bill. I just wanted to make sure – to see if our deal is still on.'

'It's on all right.'

'I love you, Gallica. That's why I came back.'

'I love *you*.'

'Promise?'

'On my mother's life.'

'There's something else?'

'What's that?' she asked anxiously.

'I seen Charles. He told me Naveed's O.K. – and he's trying the sprint tomorrow.'

'That's right.'

'I want to see it.'

'I thought – '

'I *must* see it. I want to shout for him. I want to see him win.'

'But it's tomorrow afternoon.'

'Hide me here.'

'Isn't that harbouring a criminal?'

'All right – I'll clear out.'

'I'm only joking. Come up to my room.'

'I'm filthy.'

'Have you ever had a very *quiet* bath?'

'I could try.'

'If Mum and Dad find you're here you'll be for the high jump. They'll shop you right away.'

'Where can I go? I can't take another night on the streets.'

'Wait till my parents have gone to work. Then you can have a bath.' She paused. 'We could make love afterwards.' Then she hurried on. 'Tomorrow morning I'm going to take the day off anyway so I can watch Naveed in the afternoon. So I'll lie on top of the bed – and you lie underneath.'

'What about food?'

'Can you eat flat on your back?'

'I can try.'

'When they've gone to work you can come out. Let's hope you don't get nicked on the way to school.'

'Maybe I should see you down there. I don't want you to get into trouble. They could say you were an accessory – '

'And they can say I led you, by the nose, to justice. How about that?'

They made love so rapturously that neither of them could believe it was happening. When they had finished Dex kissed her and said: 'That was worth coming home for.'

'Home? Me?'

'You're my home. Trouble is, I've got to leave it for a bit.'

'It'll be here when you get back. You're home.'

'I love you.'

'I know it's going to work out, Dex.'

'With a villain like me?'

'You'll have done your stretch.'

'I'll think about you all the time. But I don't expect you to be – not to go with anyone while I'm inside. As long as you're waiting for me when I get out.'

'I've got friends.'

'That's what I mean – '

'*Girl* friends. They'll support me. They'll keep me waiting for you.'

'But – '

'Shut up and come here.' And she drew him close.

Naveed knew that he was losing time. His feet were lead and the surface of the Hill seemed particularly shifting; it was as if the sand and gravel were trying to clutch at his feet and pull them down. He knew now that he was going to lose. It had been a long hard struggle getting fit again anyway and he still desperately missed Dex. He had almost wished he was in prison so he could be safe – so he could be serving his sentence. But on the run for so long – maybe he was dead? But somehow he had kept his voice in his mind and it was only lately that it had begun to falter – to become a thin and unrecognisable echo. A memory.

He struggled on, lifting his feet too high, knowing soon that he would look up at the top and that would be fatal. Then he heard the voice. 'Go for it.' Naveed looked down in amazement. A new, thinner, tired-looking Dex was standing there with his arm round

Gallica. 'Don't look at me,' he yelled at Naveed in the old familiar way. 'Go for it!'

Naveed went for it.

'Has he got it?' Gallica asked one of the P.E. staff.

He gave the thumbs-up sign, waving his stopwatch in the air. 'He's got it.' There was a tremendous cheer which wafted headily up to Naveed who stood on top of the Hill like a conquering hero.

'Stay where you are,' shouted up Dex.

'Why?'

'I'm giving myself up. Gallica's taking me down the nick.'

'No,' yelled Naveed. 'I want to come.'

'You stay there,' said Dex. 'You might get knocked down by a bus.' He turned to Gallica. 'Let's go.'

She put her arm through his. 'I'll be here,' she said. 'Always.'

'Let's hope it's not as long as that before I get out,' said Dex.

Naveed watched them go. For some reason he felt a surge of exultation. He began to run down the Hill.

Also by Anthony Masters

All the Fun of the Fair
(STARLING POINT 1)

Starling Point is a South London housing estate. Jim North and his Gallopers – a beautifully painted and carved fairground ride – have an annual date at the estate. But this year they have not bargained for the dramatic end of Gerry Kitson's mystery ride, nor the arrival of their new assistant, Leroy. And as Leroy desperately tries to prove himself, the battle to save the Gallopers, not only from bankruptcy but also from vandalism, begins.

Cat Burglars
(STARLING POINT 2)

CAT, is a huge Persian cat. He's Mrs Willard's pride and joy, the favourite of the twenty that live in her flat at Starling Point. He's also a ferocious menace.

When Mick Newby befriends Mrs Willard he does not know she has a secret behind the locked door in her flat. He soon discovers what it is. And when he confides in Leroy and Gallica, Mrs Willard's secret begins to invade their lives ...

Starling Point is a South London housing estate, bubbling with streetwise life. It is also the title of a series of vivid and exciting stories about the people who live there.

A selected list of titles available from Teens · Mandarin

While every effort is made to keep prices low, it is sometimes necessary to increase prices at short notice. Teens · Mandarin reserve the right to show new retail prices on covers which may differ from those previously advertised in the text or elsewhere.

The prices shown below were correct at the time of going to press.

☐	416 06252 0	**Nick's October**	Alison Prince	£1.95
☐	416 06232 6	**Haunted**	Judith St George	£1.95
☐	416 08008 0	**The Teenagers Handbook**	Murphy/Grime	£1.95
☐	416 08822 8	**The Changeover**	Margaret Mahy	£1.95
☐	416 06242 3	**I'm Not Your Other Half**	Caroline B. Cooney	£1.95
☐	416 08572 5	**Rainbows of the Gutter**	Rukshana Smith	£1.95
☐	416 03202 8	**The Burning Land**	Siegel/Siegel	£1.95
☐	416 03197 7	**Survivors**	Siegel/Siegel	£1.95
☐	416 09767 7	**Misfits**	Peggy Woodford	£1.95
☐	416 12022 9	**Picture Me Falling In Love**	June Foley	£1.95
☐	416 04022 5	**Fire and Hemlock**	Diana Wynne Jones	£1.95
☐	416 09232 2	**Short Cut to Love**	Mary Hooper	£1.95
☐	416 13102 6	**Frankie's Story**	Catherine Sefton	£1.99
☐	416 13922 1	**All the Fun of the Fair**	Anthony Masters	£1.99

All these books are available at your bookshop or newsagent, or can be ordered direct from the publisher. Just tick the titles you want and fill in the form below.

Teens · Mandarin Paperbacks, Cash Sales Department, PO Box 11, Falmouth, Cornwall TR10 9EN.

Please send cheque or postal order, no currency, for purchase price quoted and allow the following for postage and packing:

UK	55p for the first book, 22p for the second book and 14p for each additional book ordered to a maximum charge of £1.75.
BFPO and Eire	55p for the first book, 22p for the second book and 14p for each of the next seven books, thereafter 8p per book.
Overseas Customers	£1.00 for the first book plus 25p per copy for each additional book.

NAME (Block Letters) ....

ADDRESS ....

....